Praise for *Mommy's Angel*

"Miasha keeps things moving at a fast clip, but the basic empathy and understanding that pervade are the story's real appeal. [She] never loses sight of the basic humanity of all the lost souls that surround Angel."

—*Publishers Weekly*

"In the midst of all the same voices in literature, Miasha brings authenticity to the pages of this novel. She's the crème de la crème—enjoy!"

—Vickie Stringer, *Essence* bestselling author of
Let That Be the Reason

"*Mommy's Angel* highlights some of the harsh realities that many of our society's poor and forgotten children face in life. . . . Earthy, realistic, and full of unpredictable twists and turns, Miasha has written a novel that is sure to please."

—Rawsistaz.com

"*Mommy's Angel* is a fast-paced, well-written, realistic view of what addiction does to our communities. It sheds a bright light on how the addict's hurt, pain, and trouble are recycled onto the people closest to them."

—Danielle Santiago, author of *Grindin'* and the *Essence* #1 bestseller
Little Ghetto Girl

"A poignant tale of innocence lost in Brooklyn."

—K'wan, author of *Gangsta*,
Street Dreams, Eve, and *Hood Rat*

Praise for *Diary of a Mistress*

"Miasha cleverly builds up the suspense and throws in several unexpected twists. Her latest release is filled with intrigue and will keep you turning the pages. *Diary of a Mistress* will make you think twice about who you trust."

—Sheila M. Goss, e-Spire Entertainment News editor and author of *My Invisible Husband*

"Miasha has done it again. *Diary of a Mistress* is a sizzling novel full of unexpected twists and guaranteed to leave readers in shock, and gasping for air, as they excitely turn each page."

—Karen E. Quinones Miller, author of *Satin Doll, I'm Telling,* and *Satin Nights*

"*Diary of a Mistress* is an intense, captivating, and twisted love triangle. Miasha allows the usually silent mistress to raise her voice through the pages of her diary."

—Daaimah S. Poole, author of *Ex-Girl to the Next Girl, What's Real,* and *Got a Man*

"Only Miasha can make it hard to choose between wanting to be the mistress or the wife."

—Brenda L. Thomas, author of *Threesome, Fourplay,* and *The Velvet Rope*

Praise for *Secret Society*

"Scandalous and engrossing, this debut from Miasha . . . shows her to be a writer to watch."

—*Publishers Weekly*

"A sizzling and steamy novel . . . the storyline will hold readers' attention and entertain them in the process."

—*Booking Matters*

Also by Miasha

Sistah for Sale
Mommy's Angel
Diary of a Mistress
Secret Society

never enough

miasha

A TOUCHSTONE BOOK

Published by Simon & Schuster

New York   London   Toronto   Sydney

Touchstone
A Division of Simon & Schuster, Inc.
1230 Avenue of the Americas
New York, NY 10020

First Touchstone trade paperback edition July 2008

TOUCHSTONE and colophon are registered trademarks
of Simon & Schuster, Inc.

For information about special discounts for bulk purchases,
please contact Simon & Schuster Special Sales at 1-800-456-6798
or business@simonandschuster.com.

Designed by Claudia Martinez

Manufactured in the United States of America

1 3 5 7 9 10 8 6 4 2

Library of Congress Cataloging-in-Publication Data
Miasha.
Never enough / by Miasha
p. cm.
"A Touchstone book."
1. African American women—Fiction. I. Title.
PS3613.I18 N48 2008
813'.6—dc22
2007040590

ISBN-13: 978-1-4165-5338-0
ISBN-10: 1-4165-5338-X

I dedicate this one to Lorena—
your secret is safe with me.

And to all the people who asked for
Secret Society 2: *get ready.*

$\mathcal{S}$he's flatlined!" a female called out.

"Come on, Celess! Don't you die on me!" Ms. Carol, my psychiatrist, pleaded.

"What happened?" the woman asked.

"I left something at her house and when I went back to get it, I found her passed out," Ms. Carol explained, sounding horrified. "Her bottle of sedatives was empty beside her. I tried CPR on her. Then I just figured I'd better get her—"

"Possible overdose!" the woman shouted over Ms. Carol.

"Stand back!" a man ordered. "One, two, three . . ." he counted as he placed paddles on my chest. "Again!" he yelled.

All the people who ever wanted me to die didn't make it happen, including myself. Khalil put a gun to my face and pulled the trigger, and I survived. I contemplated suicide I don't know how many times in the past, but never went through with it once. And I was almost positive there were some people in the world who may have prayed for my death, maybe even my own mom, but I didn't go anywhere. However, the straw that broke the camel's back was when Michael called me months after the shooting. His voice alone gave me something to live for. He sounded so sweet and concerned when he told me he hadn't been able to stop thinking about me.

"Michael, you don't know how good it is to hear your voice," I told him, a tear sliding down my cheek. "I am so sorry. I never meant to hurt you like I did. I mean, I was playing with fire and I know that, and every time I thought about stopping it was like I couldn't, like I was addicted to the life I was leading. I can't explain it. It's so difficult to be someone you're not and go your whole life trying to hide who you really are. All I know is that I was wrong and I wish it didn't take for me to get shot in the face and my best friend to get killed for me to learn that lesson."

I had to pause to slow up my crying and then I continued, "For what it's worth, I deeply apologize for deceiving you. You didn't deserve to be done like that, honestly, and believe me I am getting my payback. Not a day goes by that I don't think about killing myself. It's just painful, the whole thing. I can't really explain it. All I can do is keep apologizing and beg for your forgiveness."

"Are you finished?" Michael's saddened voice asked considerately.

I was crying too much to answer; besides, I didn't want to. I was anxious about what he had to say. I clutched the phone tighter and pressed it against my ear harder just to be sure I could hear him clearly. I wanted to feel like I was next to him, like he was right there on my couch, my head leaning on his broad shoulder.

"I don't know where to start," he began. "I mean, you hurt me. You hurt me bad. I can't even tell you how much it hurts. I put a lot into you, Celess. I was a damn good man to you. I opened you that salon. I just knew you were going to be the woman I made my wife." Then, anger building in his tone, he said, "But you completely destroyed all of that. You destroyed my life and you know what, I feel bad that Tina died and you didn't. Both of you were trifling, lying bitches and both of you should be burning in hell right now! You talk about killing yourself, go ahead. Even the score. You were going to leave me and move to L.A. with Tina so you might as well go to hell with her too! Think about it—don't you deserve the same punishment as her? You were both doing the same thing, running around in skirts and makeup telling guys like me you were women when you were really men. You disgust me, Celess! I really, really hope that you do commit suicide. That's the only way I'd know for sure that your ass would be burning in hell where you belong. So go ahead! Don't talk about it, be about it. Soon as I hang this phone up in your ear, slit your fucking wrist, go jump off a bridge, anything. I don't give a fuck. You could die right now and I wouldn't shed a single tear. I hate you for what you did to me! Kill yourself, bitch!" *Click.*

That did it. No one and nothing had done it up to that point. But Michael had pushed me to my limit. Of all people, he was the only one who had the power to bring an end to my life. Khalil couldn't do it with a thirty-eight. But Michael did it with his words.

The Introduction

Flashbacks of my life appeared in my thoughts. Tina's pretty smile, money, cars, designer clothes, jewelry, and the men—oh, the men! I think I might have been smiling in the hospital bed when I thought about the men. Their sexy asses. I couldn't believe the turn my life had taken. I couldn't believe I was up in the hospital once again having doctors fight to save my life. What was going to come of all this, I didn't know. Was I facing life or death? I wondered. And if I was to survive this one, what would I do differently? How would I live my life? I felt myself regaining consciousness as more thoughts filled my head.

"Celess," I heard a woman's voice mumble. It grew louder. "CELESS!"

I opened my eyes slowly and blinked several times trying to adjust to the bright lights. Ms. Carol was standing over me.

"She's awake!" Ms. Carol shouted.

A nurse entered the room and began waving her hands in front of my face. Naturally, my eyes followed her hands and that was a for-sure sign that I was no longer in a comatose state. Days later, right before my discharge, Ms. Carol came to see me and try to talk some sense into me.

"So," she said, shaking her head back and forth. "What are you going to do, live the rest of your life in and out of the hospital, pitying yourself?"

"That's not what I want," I answered, depressed.

"Then what do you want?"

"I want my life back. The way it was before."

"Well, I don't know about that, Celess. I mean, you weren't living right before and that's why you're suffering now."

"I know. So really it's not up to me. It's karma."

"But you can change all of that," she said, reaching into her pocketbook. "I've been doing some research and I found out that men who go through with the sex change tend to have happier lives post-op than pre-op."

I looked at the pamphlets Ms. Carol had in her hands and didn't say anything.

"I just think you should do it. I know you want to be a woman more than anything, and you have so much more living to do. This is your second brush with death because of the same thing. How much longer are you going to allow this dark cloud to hang over you? And how many more times do you think God is going to spare your life?" Ms. Carol pressed.

I thought about what Ms. Carol was saying and she was right. I *did* want to be a woman. But I was letting my situation get the best of me. I was letting sadness and depression take control of me, and I was actually getting used to sympathy. Maybe I was pitying myself, and that was no way to live for somebody like me, who'd loved life at one time.

Ms. Carol interrupted my thoughts. "You're so young, Celess. You're only twenty-two years old. You have a full life ahead of you. Why let it waste away?"

I finally spoke. "All right. I want to do it."

Ms. Carol's face lit up. "Are you serious?" she asked. "I mean, by no means do I want you to go through with this on my account. I want it to be something *you* really want to do."

"Ms. Carol, I'm tired of living this way. You're right, I'm only twenty-two. I could be doing so much, seeing so much, being so much. If it was meant for me to die, I would have been dead. God must have a plan for me. And who am I to disrupt that?"

Ms. Carol nodded and with tears in her eyes she said, "I just think you'll be so happy. I can see you being this beautiful woman with so much to offer this world."

"Well, whatever the outcome, I'm tired of risking my life for one organ. Cut the shit off," I said plainly.

Ms. Carol went on to explain the procedure and the costs based on her research. She even gave me the names and numbers of a few surgeons. Most were out of town, but they were specialists and had achieved optimum results. When it was all said and done, I took Ms. Carol's advice. I left the hospital with a mission to accomplish. I was going to be a woman once and for all.

Getting sexual reassignment surgery, or SRS, took a lot more than what I initially expected. I thought I could research a surgeon, schedule an appointment, and have it done. That was *so* not the case. I was ordered to be evaluated by a psychiatrist for six months—luckily, I had Ms. Carol—and a medical doctor had to determine me a suitable candidate according to the guidelines of the Harry Benjamin International Gender Dysphoria Association. In the meantime, I opted to go ahead and get the facial feminizing surgery I had discussed with my doctor in the past. I had the forehead surgery, which included scalp advancement, brow elevation, the removal of my superorbital bossing, and the contouring of my orbital rim. I also had a rhinoplasty, otherwise known as a nose job. I waited a month to have a cheek augmentation. Then I got hair transplants. I had just completed my genital electrolysis and was ready for my actual sex change, or a vaginoplasty, as it's called in medical terms. Along with that procedure I was getting a boob job the same day. I stored my sperm in case in the future I wanted to have a baby. I didn't think I would—especially not with *my* sperm—but when the option was presented to me, I said what the hell, you never know.

I was nervous going into the surgery, even after undergoing so many others beforehand. But this was the big one, the one that would forever make me a woman. There was no turning back. I spent about nine days in the hospital after having my penis inverted to create a vagina. Then three months later I was back in for the follow-up procedure, the labioplasty, where the doctor basically perfected the form and look of my new sex. The next day I was on my way back home to Philly from Portland, Oregon. I had my name changed legally as well as my Social Security number.

It took close to two long, gruesome years before I was done with all my surgeries and I officially became Celess. It took me a little while to get fully comfortable in my new skin. Actually, it seemed like I would never get there. I mean, don't get me wrong—I was pleased with the results. I looked pretty like I had before I was shot in the face. And my body was right. It was just that I was still self-conscious. I guessed it was because of having been cooped up in the house for so long, and then whenever I did go outside I wasn't receiving attention from men like I used to. A casual hello or a minor glance was all I got; the stop-and-stare and the turning heads were a thing of the past. Maybe it was me, but I kept asking myself had I made a mistake. Had I lost my sex appeal when I lost my penis? I didn't know. But what I did know was that I was bound to be one miserable tranny if shit didn't change soon.

Ms. Carol invited me on a shopping trip to Woodbury

Commons, an outlet mall of high-end stores in upstate New York. I didn't want to go, partly because I didn't do the outlet shopping shit and partly because I hadn't been in the mood to go anywhere since my transformation. But she practically begged me, and when I thought about it, I realized I could use some lounge-around clothes and I did need some new bras for my recently enhanced bustline. So I decided to go. It was a good thing too, because it was there that I met Brad, a New York City–based photographer. He was eyeing me while I selectively picked through the marked-down items in Dolce & Gabbana. He approached me and handed me his business card.

"Excuse me for intruding, but I couldn't help but notice your stunning beauty," he said with what sounded like a Russian accent.

I smiled and took the card. Not that I cared what it said or who he was. But the fact that he was the first guy to compliment me in such a way in such a long time made me feel open. Shit, I could have fallen in love with him right then and there.

"I'm a fashion photographer and I'm actually in the process of shooting an editorial for *Harper's Bazaar* magazine—"

"I love *Bazaar*," I cut him off. I was overexcited and maybe even a little fake, but I couldn't help it. I could not keep my cool with the guy.

"Yeah? Well, I'd love it if you could come and do a test shoot for it. I think your look is just perfect for the story."

"Well, here, take my number," I said, almost throwing myself at him. "Call me. I'll do it."

I gave the photographer my cell phone number and got back to shopping. I didn't have any expectations and figured if he called, he called. Shit, I was just happy he called me beautiful.

I heard from Brad a couple days later and took the train to New York that following week. It was right before Christmas in 2004.

"Hold that, yes. Great. That's beautiful." Brad guided me as he snapped away. "Last frame."

I exhaled after the last flash sparked. It had been one long day in New York. Scene after scene, wardrobe change after wardrobe change, shot after shot. I was exhausted to say the least, but my adrenaline was pumping.

"How did I do?" I asked Brad.

"Just as I expected," he responded. "Fantastic. You can get changed."

I smiled at Brad's report and headed toward the changing room. Inside were two guys who were apparently getting ready for their photo shoot. They looked up and greeted me as I entered. Then they continued doing what they were doing before I walked in. I waited a few seconds before grabbing my clothes off the hangers to see if they would offer me privacy. When they didn't I figured I was expected to change in front of them. The nervousness quickly evaporated as I remembered I had nothing to hide anymore. I was a woman with a well-constructed vagina, and, in fact, I was eager to show it off. I hadn't gotten any opinions on it from people other than doctors and nurses, so a positive reaction from the guys in the dressing room would be a morale booster.

I pulled off the big fluffy dress I was in, took down my panty hose, and slipped into my jeans panty-less. I noticed the guys peeking and I smiled inside at their obvious hard-ons. I felt myself growing confident and horny at the same time. Then I thought of having a threesome with them. Hell, they were good-looking young models—possibly even the next Tyson Beckfords. Fucking them while they were still undiscovered could be an investment in my future.

Just as I was fantasizing about a sexual escapade, reality set in. I started asking myself all kinds of crazy questions: *What if your vagina isn't ready to be penetrated yet? What if your walls come crashing down? You know you can't naturally get wet like that. What if it hurts real bad?* I was tripping myself out pondering all the what-ifs. Meanwhile, the two guys were sending flirtatious glances at me like they were sex deprived and I was the last woman on earth. I figured I had two options— test my new parts out on strangers who if all went wrong I'd never have to see again, or wait until I got into a relationship with a guy and let him take me for a test drive. It made more sense to go with the strangers. Hell, I done had my share of so-called lovers finding out about my secret. If I was going to get involved with someone, I needed all my shit to be in perfect working order.

I ended up letting one of the guys test out my new parts while the other fucked me in the ass, which was tight since I hadn't had any in so long. It felt like I was a virgin all over again. I won't lie, it was awkward as hell and painful, but as my nerves eased and my mind got into it, I was lovin' it like I used to.

I guess Brad grew suspicious when I hadn't exited the changing room as quickly as I should have. Who knows? He probably had his ear to the door listening to my moans the way he barged into the dressing room like he already knew something was going on. I just knew the guys and I were in for a cursing out. I mean, we basically turned Brad's studio into HBO's *Cathouse*. Instead, he asked if he could join the fun. It would have been rather rude for me to turn him down, so I gave him some too. A few days later I got a call from Brad saying that I was chosen to shoot for *Bazaar* above six professional models.

I didn't hesitate returning to New York, and I didn't hesitate fucking Brad once more either. As far as I was concerned, it was that act that got me the gig. Instantly, my mind started to catch up to my body and I was turning back into Celess. My old theory about using what you got to get what you want resurfaced, and I found a new business to apply it to.

After my photo appeared in such a major fashion publication, I started getting more print work. From there I landed some runway jobs. I wasn't the best walker, but I was damn good on my knees and I ended up doing two shows during New York Fashion Week in February 2005. I was raking in the dough and making a name for myself at the same time. Nothing could be better. I told Ms. Carol that it was all blessings bestowed upon me, leaving out the extra things I was doing to get where I was. I figured it was none of her business what I did behind closed doors.

People were buzzing about me in the fashion industry, and by the summer I had a professional portfolio and was offered a contract with an elite modeling agency in California. I immediately started making plans to relocate. I put my house on the market and started calling all the utility companies I had accounts with to schedule shut-off dates. In the process, I realized that if and when my mom decided to return my calls, she wouldn't get through if I had my house phone cut off. So a day before the scheduled shut-off date, I called her once more. I left a message on her machine telling her of my newfound success and my upcoming move to L.A. I let her know that she needed to call me quickly before my phone was disconnected. Surprisingly, she finally reached out to me. I didn't know if it was because I had told her that I was about to be famous or if she just wanted to see me before I left for L.A. Either way, she arranged for me to visit her the day before my flight out.

I walked up to my old house; my mom was out front gardening. Her back was turned to me as I went up the steps. Her lime green short-sleeve shirt and matching lime green capris were a bit tight; I could see that she had put on a few pounds. My mom wasn't what you would call a skinny minnie anymore. I had tears in my eyes, looking at how slowly she was moving compared to how she did when I was a kid watching her tend to our lawn. It made me realize just how much time had gone by since I had seen her last—how much of her life I'd missed out on.

"You still have the best flowers on the block," I said.

"Charles?" my mom asked, without turning around.

I held out my hands, palms turned up, and replied, "What's left of 'im."

My mom turned around to see just what was left of her only son, and her eyes zoomed in on me. She looked me over: starting at my fresh layered weave, making her way down to my white-and-silver Dior tee, faded black Hudson jeans, and finally my silver Dior flip-flops. Standing stiff, tears running down her face, she shook her head.

"Charles, look at you."

I didn't say anything—I didn't know how she was taking my transformation. Was she still upset or just surprised? I wasn't sure, so I just stood there quietly waiting to find out.

"What did you do to yourself?" she asked, removing her gloves.

"Well," I said, not knowing what else to say. "I got a sex change." I stated the obvious.

My mom shook her head again and wiped her eyes.

"Why did you come here, Charles? Why did you even bother?" she asked.

I put my hands down back to my sides and let go of the tears that were waiting patiently in the corners of my eyes.

"Because I thought that somehow deep in your heart you would have unconditional love for me like I have for you," I answered her. "But," I said before she could say anything else, "I guess not. Sorry for disturbing you." I turned around and walked back down the steps. My mom watched me as I got inside my rented Dodge Charger.

"Unconditional love is one thing, eternal love is another. At some point you have to pray for eternal love, and doing what you're doing, you'll never get it," my mom reminded me.

"Good-bye, Mom," I said, starting up the car. With tears streaming down my face I vowed, "I'm going to Hollywood and I'ma be a big star. You don't have to love me. But I guarantee you, the whole world will." I pulled away from the curb and promised myself that that was the last time I would try to make amends with my mom. I washed my hands of her.

Fourteen Months Later . . .
September 2006

_O_ooh, I love it!" I squealed, looking at the 1,900-square-foot condo in downtown L.A.

"You like it, really?" Terry asked. "I know it's not as big as my brother's house, but it's only you, you know?"

"Oh, please. Like I expect you to put me in my own mansion. It'll do just fine," I said, hugging him and kissing him on his cheek.

Terry was an older, white, filthy rich investor I used to mess with. I met him through my best friend, Tina, who was messing with his twin brother, Derrek. Tina actually ended up marrying Derrek but due to her untimely death, their marriage was short-lived. However, Derrek kept in touch with me over the years, even contributing largely to my surgery. When I first moved out to the West Coast, I stayed with him. I would have stayed with Terry, seeing as how he was the one I used to deal with, but at the time he had a woman living with him. From what I got out of Derrek one night when he was drunk, she was a trans-prostitute Terry had picked up and pretty-womaned. I didn't care, though. I never did like Terry. He wasn't attractive and being bald, old, and flabby didn't help. Plus, when I did have a dick he liked for me to fuck him in the ass rather than the other way around, and I wasn't into that. I only did it because he was peeling me off.

"So Derrek and I are going to help you furnish the place," Terry said, walking behind me as I toured my new place.

"Where's he at, anyway? I thought he was meeting us here," I said.

"He was, but he called. One of his meetings ran over. But he told me to tell you that he hopes you like it. He went through a lot to get it. One of his colleagues had it under contract. He had to almost triple the value to get him to cut it loose."

"Well, you tell him that I absolutely love it! And I can't explain how grateful I am to him for doing this for me. You both have been lifesavers for me."

"Don't mention it. It's what we do, you know?" Terry said modestly. Looking at his watch, he asked, "What time are the movers coming with your things?"

"They said between one and four," I said, looking at my cell phone to check the time.

"Well, it's a quarter to three so they should be here soon. I'm going to get outta here, though. I have to pick up Andrea from the doctor's."

I acted concerned. "Is everything all right?" I asked.

Terry nodded. "Just Botox, that's all."

"Oh, okay," I said. "Well, I'm going to start wiping down everything so when the movers come they can just put things in place."

"You should have told Derrek to send Lucille by. She would have cleaned the place spotless."

"No, it's fine. You two have done enough. The least I can do is clean my own spot."

"Well, have fun," Terry joked. "I'll call you later."

"All right. Thanks again," I said, hugging Terry once more.

He kissed me on my lips. Once he disappeared, I did amateur cartwheels throughout the open living room. I was ecstatic to have such a big condo downtown. It was my dream house complete with all the modern amenities one could wish for. *Terry and Derrek outdid themselves*, I thought. They'd always been big spenders and after I was shot and Tina was killed, they felt sorry for me. And even though what happened to us wasn't their fault, I guess their extreme generosity was their way of saying sorry. *Keep the apologies coming, motherfuckers*, I thought, smiling ear to ear, looking around at my new home. *Keep the apologies coming!*

A few weeks passed before my condo was fully furnished. I chose black leather for my seating and glass tops for my tables.

I did a winter white alpaca rug on the floor and a couple of expensive paintings on the walls. I kept the decor simple. I didn't want to clutter the open space. When I was done playing interior designer, I grew bored with myself. I decided that now that I was out on my own and actually had rent to pay, I needed to book more gigs. My agency was passing things off to me like small-time runway shows and functions and some low-budget advertisements, but I didn't travel all the way to the opposite side of the country to be mediocre. Shit, I would have been better off in New York.

I decided that I would take matters into my own hands. I knew that physical appearance was the first thing clients looked at when choosing models, and even though I was naturally thin, in Hollywood that meant nothing. Everybody was thin. You had to be toned as well. I got a membership at an upscale gym that was known for accommodating celebrities. The fees were a hefty sum to add to my already expensive lifestyle, but I figured it would be worth it. I started working out three days a week. Eventually I hired a trainer—or, should I say, I used the barter system to obtain a trainer. His name was Corey. He had trained the best of the best. And from the looks of it, he was in the greatest shape of them all. I didn't know how to measure his abs, but he was definitely past a six-pack. His arms looked like boulders, chiseled to perfection. And his legs were long and athletic, making him appear taller than he actually was.

"When will I start seeing results?" I asked, examining my

abs in the floor-to-ceiling mirror in Corey's personal gym. We had just completed a workout and I was dying to see the fruits of my labor.

Corey walked over to me and ran his finger across my stomach. "You don't see those muscles forming?" he asked.

"Stop, that tickles," I told him, chuckling.

"Well, would you rather it hurt?" he asked, pushing up on me.

"What are you suggesting?" I asked, backing up.

Corey pulled me to him by the elastic waist on my stretch pants. "One more workout," he said seductively.

"Right here?" I asked.

"Right now," he responded.

Corey then initiated a long and succulent kiss, which led to me giving him oral sex in front of the mirror I was just checking myself out in. After becoming completely aroused, Corey picked me up off my knees and pulled down my stretch pants and thong. He rubbed my ass with his big, muscular hands and then retrieved a condom from his back pocket. As he slid the rubber over his erect penis, he instructed me to play with myself. I licked my fingers and started rubbing them up and down my clitoris. Bent over, I braced myself for Corey's grand entrance. His thing was well in proportion with his body. It was huge.

"Aaahhh," I squealed as he entered me. "Go slow, baby!"

"I'm not going to hurt you," he said, stroking me from behind.

"Corey! Corey!" I shouted, boosting his ego and apparently his stamina too because he started moving faster and faster.

"Oh my God!" I yelled out. "You killin' it!" I added.

My face was scrunched and my eyes were watering as Corey thrust what felt like a whole arm in and out of me. See, what he didn't know was that my depth wasn't equivalent to an average female's. In a transsexual, the size of your penis determined how deep your vagina would be. I wouldn't let him know that, of course. But the fact of the matter was, I dreaded having sex with Corey. He was big enough as it was, and my situation just made it worse.

"Please cum! Please cum! Please cum!" I panted, feeling the walls of my vagina expand with force. And as I begged, Corey went faster and harder. He got a kick out of "banging my back out," as he called it. He thought it was cute. I, on the other hand, could have gone without. There's a fine line between good big dick and just big dick, and what lived in his pants was walking that line. It was monstrous. I took it, though. I had to. It was the only way I'd be able to afford his ass.

"Thank you!" I gasped as Corey's body began to tremble and his movements finally slowed down to a halt.

"I'm sorry," he said, pulling out of me. "I can't help it. Every time you start cheerleading, I start thinking about the days that I used to play football. I just be in the zone, tearing through you like the great running back I am," Corey boasted.

"Whatever, nigga," I said, clutching my stomach with one

hand and pulling my panties up with the other. "All I know is I'm gonna need a doctor if you keep fuckin' me so hard. I'm not a gang of husky niggas tryin' to tackle you, and my pussy is not an end zone."

Corey chuckled as he walked to the bathroom to flush the condom. I pulled my pants up and followed him. Inside the tiny restroom, I wiped myself with a wet paper towel. Then I washed my hands while Corey peed.

"Today was on the house," Corey said.

"Oh really?" I asked rhetorically. "I wonder why."

"Even exchange." He smiled.

"So, technically, it wasn't on the house," I said.

"Well, you know," he said, still wearing a grin.

Buzz. The buzzer to Corey's leased space interrupted our small talk.

"You expectin' somebody?" I asked.

"My next appointment," he said.

"Male or female?" I asked.

"Male, why?" he asked back, going for the door.

"Just curious," I said, leaving the bathroom behind him.

"I know we're not jealous."

"Me? Of course not," I said.

"Yeah, all right. You know how y'all get after a power shot. Y'all start gettin' real curious," Corey teased.

"It is not that serious," I said.

Corey opened the door. He spoke to his next appointment, another well-built, handsome chocolate man. Then he turned back to me to get in the last word. "Oh, it's serious," he boasted.

I just smiled and waited to be introduced to the unknown guy who had just walked in. Corey returned the smile and did the honors. "Celess, this is another trainee of mine, Sean, Sean, Celess."

"Nice to meet you," I said, rather flirtatiously. I wanted to tug at Corey's bootstraps a bit and remind him who was in charge.

"The pleasure is mine," Sean said, just as flirtatious.

"Damn," Corey said. "Y'all might as well just fuck right here."

Sean frowned like Corey was speaking something other than English. Me, I just laughed.

"See you tomorrow, Corey," I said, walking out the door.

"Maybe," Corey said with a playful attitude.

I got inside my BMW 3 series coupe. I threw my gym bag in the backseat and tuned the radio to 93.5 to see what Steve Harvey and them was trippin' about that morning. I was driving through the thick rush hour traffic headed back to my condo when I got a call on my cell.

"Hello," I answered, turning down the volume on my radio.

"Celess," Corey's voice sounded.

"What's up?"

"Listen, Sean, the guy I just introduced you to, is producing a music video and they're casting the female lead. He said that you had a good look for the girl if you wanna audition for it."

The first thing I thought was that it was some ol' rinky-dink video for an unknown artist. "Whose video is it?" I asked to confirm my suspicions.

"Whose video is it?" Corey repeated my question; his voice was kind of muffled, so I figured he was talking to Sean. "It's for Chris Brown."

Okay, I thought, impressed. *But what's the catch?* They probably wanted me to be some hoochie in the video turning little Chris Brown out. And it wasn't that I would mind turning Chris Brown out—shit, he was a sexy-ass little young bull. Plus, he was making some paper. But it was just that I had to be smart out here in Hollywood. I couldn't jump at every opportunity if it meant it would prevent me from getting others.

"Will I be like a video vixen type or will it be a classier role?" I asked.

"Naw," Corey said. "You would be like the main girl."

"Oh, well then hell yeah I wanna audition. When and where?" I asked.

"You got a pen?"

"Actually, you know what, I'm driving. Can you call me right back and leave the information on my voice mail?"

"Yeah, I can do that."

"All right, that'll work. Good lookin' out, Corey."

"No problem. You see what I do for you, even after you tried to play me?"

"What are you talkin' about? I would never try to play you." I acted innocent.

"Yeah, I bet." Corey didn't buy it. "Anyway, let me go. I'll holla at you."

"Call me right back and leave the information," I reiterated.

"Yeah, I am."

"All right."

"All right. 'Bye."

Seconds later, my phone rang again. I pressed the Ignore button to send the call straight to my voice mail. I felt giddy about the possibility of being the main chick in a Chris Brown video. He was fairly new to the industry, but he was the shit. I was sure that getting that gig would open up many more doors for me.

"Ms. Carol, I got it!" I screamed in the phone.

"You did?!" Ms. Carol asked, just as excited.

"Yeah! I just got off the phone with the casting agent!"

"Oh, my goodness, congratulations!"

"Thank you."

"So tell me all about it," she said.

"Well, first of all I had to audition at a warehouse in West

Hollywood. They basically wanted me to walk, and they played his song. They gave me some little scenarios to act out without dialogue. And they took some pictures of me and a video of me . . ."

"Were you nervous?" Ms. Carol asked.

"No. I thought I would be. But they were so cool they made me feel comfortable. As soon as I walked in the room they were oohin' and aahin' talking about how pretty I was."

"I am so happy for you!"

"Thank you so much."

"So when do you start taping?" Ms. Carol asked, obviously not up on the industry jargon.

"We start shooting in two weeks," I said.

"Well, congratulations again, sweetie."

"Thanks. Well, let me call you back. There's somebody on my other line and I don't know who it is."

"Oh okay, go ahead. I'll talk to you later."

"All right." I ended my call with Ms. Carol and clicked over.

"Celess?"

"Yes, this is she," I replied.

"Hi, this is Sean. I met you that day when you were leaving Corey's gym."

"Oh, yeah, hey Sean."

"Hey, what's up. I'm just calling you to congratulate you on getting the part for the video."

"Oh, that's sweet. Thank you so much," I said, still smiling from talking to Ms. Carol.

"You're welcome. I guess I'll see you on the set," Sean said.

"Yes, you will."

"All right then, I'm looking forward to it," he said. "Corey's told me a lot about you," he added.

"Well I hope it was all good," I said.

"Oh, most definitely," he said. "I actually can't wait to see for myself."

"Are you flirting again?" I came out and asked. It was clear to me that he was—no sense in beating around the bush.

"I guess you can call it that. You know, I put a good word in to the casting director."

"So was it me or you who got me the role?"

"Both."

"So I guess I owe you one, huh?" I asked, cutting to the chase.

"Well . . ." he mumbled.

"I got you," I said. "No need for you to be speechless. If you want something you have to ask for it, right? And ain't shit for free. If I ain't learned anything from being out here a whole year, I've learned those two things."

"Well, since you put it like that . . ." he said.

"Listen, I appreciate whatever you did to get me the role,

and if I have to return the favor then I will," I told him bluntly.

"I must say, Ms. Celess, with that attitude and your looks, you can make it quite far out here."

"Well, that's been my goal since I stepped off the plane, Mr. Sean," I informed him.

"I like you."

"I like you too," I said softly.

"What are you doing this evening?"

"Nothing as of yet."

"How about we go grab something to eat?"

"I'd like that."

"I'll pick you up at about seven. Does that work for you?"

"It most certainly does. Let me give you my address."

"You know what, I'm driving home from the office. Why don't you call me right back and leave it on my voice mail?"

"Are you mocking me?" I joked.

"No, I just know what works," he assured me.

"How about I text it to you?"

"That's even better."

"All right."

"My number should have come up in your phone."

I took my phone away from my ear briefly and looked at the screen. "It did," I confirmed.

"All right. I'll await your text."

"Okay."

"'Bye."

"'Bye."

My dinner date with Sean along with my role in Chris Brown's video was just the boost my career needed. I ended up doing more videos and raking in more dough, *and* I was officially dating Sean, who had gotten me a significant role in an independent short film. My life was improving quickly, and things were finally falling into place for me in L.A. I was soon able to live comfortably off of booking jobs, not to mention the few dollars I was getting for fucking a couple guys every so often. And with Derrek and Terry still helping me out, my bank account rose rapidly, and if you know me you know that money turned me on the most. Fuck a man with a big dick. Seeing doubles and triples of that old fat-ass Benjamin Franklin was enough to give me multiple orgasms.

Before long, I had become a stereotypical L.A. girl. I carried my head high and my nose to the clouds. I kept myself together in the latest and most expensive shit I could find. My hair, nails, and makeup never needed to be done and I even started tanning—not much, though. I was light-skinned, but I was still black so all I needed every now and again was a spray-on. The best part about all of it was that

I wasn't paranoid. I was getting money and having my way with niggas like I used to, but this time without the hassle of trying to hide a dick. If I knew years ago what I know now, I would have been *cut it off*. Maybe then Tina would still be alive.

October 2006

I was minding my business in a boutique in the Beverly Center when one of the girls who worked there approached me.

"Hi, can I help you find something?" the girl asked.

"No, thank you," I said with slight attitude, wondering how she thought she could help me. I mean, I was in a pair of Rock & Republic skinny jeans, black patent leather Christian Louboutins with the cork platform, and a fitted black-and-gold Rock & Republic zip-up jacket, *and* I was carrying an oversize YSL black patent leather bag accented with gold hardware. I clearly did not need help picking out hot shit.

"We just got these in," she said, picking up a pair of Allen B. jeans. "Nobody has them yet."

"Oh, okay," I said, growing frustrated.

"Oh, and these would be hot on you. What are you, like a

twenty-four, twenty-six?" she asked, measuring me with her eyes.

"How much are they?" I asked, agitated.

She looked at the tag and said, "One eighty-five."

"Jeans less than five hundred don't fit me right," I said, rolling my eyes.

I thought that would give her the message to go nag somebody the hell else. But she didn't. Instead, her pesky ass kept talking.

"Oh, you gettin' money, huh?" she asked.

"Is that a trick question?" I asked, not even looking at the girl.

"No. It's actually a compliment. I'm tryna be right there with you."

I stopped perusing and finally looked at the girl. She was tall, maybe a couple inches taller than my five-foot-six stance. She was light-skinned with yellow undertones and had blond and brown hair. She looked like she was mixed with something and had big titties like most of the girls in L.A. Her style was cute, just inexpensive-looking. Overall, though, she was put together nicely. *Hell, she just might make a perfect sidekick*, I thought. *She definitely complements me*. And it was apparent she had thick-enough skin and persistence.

I figured I'd test her. "You down for runnin' G on niggas?" I asked her straight-up.

"What you mean?" She put on a puzzled look.

"Fuckin' guys for money." I was blunt with the young girl. No need in beating around the bush. Either I would shut her up once and for all and get back to shopping, or I would acquire a teammate.

"Oh, that's what I do best," she surprisingly replied.

I reached in my pocketbook and pulled out one of my business cards. It wasn't for the business we were discussing, of course, but it had my number on it. I handed it to the girl and told her to call me whenever she quit her job.

Without taking my card, she walked over to the counter where another girl was stationed and got her attention. "Nikki," she said. "Tell Lou I quit."

Then the girl walked back toward me and said, "I quit."

She was ambitious like a motherfucker. I liked that. She reminded me somewhat of Tina. She was a go-getter indeed and even seemed to be a rider.

"Let's bounce then," I told her, putting down the pair of Rogan jeans I was contemplating buying.

"Si-Si, where are you going?" the girl Nikki called out as we exited the store.

"I said I quit!" she yelled.

"So ya name is Si-Si?" I asked, a smirk on my face.

"Yeah. What's yours?"

"Celess," I told her.

"Nice to meet you," she said, shaking my hand.

"You crazy as hell, Si-Si," I told her, chuckling.

"You just don't know how bad I was waitin' for an opportunity like this. I've been tryin' to catch a break. But it's all about who you know out here, you know? And I'm not from here, so I don't know nobody. Then I seen you, all flashy and shit, and you was shoppin' without a man, which is unusual, especially spendin' the type of money you were talkin' about. I figured I had to know you and be down with whatever you had goin' on. That's why I was on ya heels in the store. I don't usually do that," Si-Si explained off the bat.

"Oh, well, that's good to know. Because that shit was pissin' me off," I admitted.

"I know. It pisses me off when people do that shit to me."

"All right, so now that we got past that and we're on a first-name basis, what's next? I mean, what do you have to do for the rest of the day?"

"Well I don't have to work until nine anymore, so I guess I got the rest of the day free," she said sarcastically.

"You're cuttin' into my shopping time, but I *am* hungry, so how about we sit down and grab some lunch?" I suggested.

"That sounds good to me," Si-Si said. "And as for your shopping, shit, I can be a big help to you. I know this mall like the back of my hand. Plus, I know people at all the hot stores. I can get you discounts for days."

My kind of girl, I thought, getting excited. But then I piped down. Who was this chick? She could have been a serial killer or a thievin'-ass junkie for all I knew. She could have been setting me up or some shit. I didn't know. And I was walking through the mall with her ass, about to have lunch with her like she was my best friend. I was tripping a little bit.

"You ever eat at Grand Lux?" Si-Si asked, interrupting my rational thoughts.

"Hell yeah! They got the best food in this mall!" My mouth started watering, and the thoughts I was having about Si-Si turned into thoughts of me sinking my teeth in some grilled salmon.

"Don't they?" she agreed. "You wanna eat there?"

"Yeah. I can go for one of their lunch specials."

Si-Si and I were seated at a booth. After we ordered our drinks and entrees we got to the bottom of who we each were and what we planned to get from each other. Let's face it, we didn't know each other well enough to care for each other, so our friendship or partnership or whatever you wanted to call it was definitely founded on ulterior motives.

"So," I began. "You said that fuckin' guys for money is what you do best. Then why ain't you been doin' it?"

"First of all, it's not something I wanna do or even like to do, but it seems to be the thing I'm best at," Si-Si said quite frankly.

"That brings me back to my question," I said. "Why haven't you been doin' it?"

"To be honest, I never knew where to start," she responded.

"Plus, I have trust issues. I don't trust no fuckin' body, especially no men."

"Well, you just upped and quit your job on an assumption that I, a perfect stranger, would put you on some money. That's pretty damn trusting, if you ask me—maybe *too* damn trusting," I told her.

"Yeah, but you being a chick sat better with me than it would have had you been a dude. Actually, I wouldn't even have approached you if you was a dude or if you was with a dude. And anyway I'm desperate now and I don't have much more to lose."

"How long have you been out here?" I probed.

"Since oh-four," Si-Si said.

"Shit, you got out here just a year before me."

Just then our waiter brought our drinks. He placed the pineapple juice in front of me and the strawberry lemonade in front of Si-Si.

"So, how did you make your come-up so quick?" Si-Si asked, sipping her juice.

"Fuckin' guys." I chuckled as if to say *I told you already.* "What, you thought I was playin'?"

"No. But I just thought there was more to the story."

"Well, I do some modeling and acting," I revealed.

"That's what I really wanna get into," Si-Si said, passion in her eyes.

"Don't every pretty girl out here?"

"Basically. But I've wanted to be an actress since I was a little girl. It's not like I'm just tryna to get famous and make an easy buck. It's really something I've always dreamt of doing," Si-Si expressed fervently.

"So what stopped you?"

"It just seems like it's a name game out here. If you can't tell a casting director the name of a person who referred you then you can pretty much forget it."

I nodded and sipped my pineapple juice. "That seems to be mostly the case," I agreed.

"So how did you get your start?" she asked.

"Actually, I shot an editorial for *Bazaar* back in New York and things kind of took off for me since then. I got a contract with Shiner Modeling Agency and moved out here."

"Shiner? Are you serious?" she asked, eyes wide in amazement.

"Yeah, and how you look is exactly how I felt when I got it. But that gettin' signed shit don't really make the difference. I mean, it helps, yeah, but gettin' big gigs does take a little extra."

"Yeah? You would think that once you get with a big agency like Shiner you would be set."

"That's where most people make their mistake. It takes even more drive and determination because gettin' signed to a major agency just makes you a small fish in a big pond."

"Oh, that makes sense," Si-Si said, feasting her eyes on something past me. "That must be ours."

I turned to look behind me and a tray of the most delicious-looking food was within my reach. The waiter carefully took each dish off the tray and placed them on our table. Both Si-Si and I were looking at the food like we hadn't eaten in months. No sooner had the waiter put the last dish on the table than Si-Si and me dug in.

Having lunch with Si-Si and getting to know her made me feel like we could indeed be friends. She was witty like me and quick on her toes. We had a lot in common. Plus, she was a rider with a big heart. I learned that she lived with her mom and grandmother in a two-bedroom apartment in Pasadena. She didn't have kids or a man and had somewhat of a wild past. I told her that I too had a wild past, but neither of us got into too much detail. She said she came out to L.A. with a lot of paper and even more ambition, spending every bit of 200K on acting schools, coaches, photographers, and every other scheming opportunist L.A. was flooded with. Eventually, the ambition outlived the paper and she been working odd jobs to take care of herself and her peoples. Recently, her grandmom got sick and that was when she became more desperate for money. She needed to find a way to pay for her grandmom's care. At that, her being overzealous was justified; I understood her position.

"I got it," Si-Si said, sliding the bill over to her side of the table.

"You sure?" I asked.

"Yeah," she said, wiping the corners of her mouth with her napkin.

I was impressed by Si-Si's offering to pay the tab, even though she probably didn't have it to spare. I made a promise to myself that I would look out for her and show her how to make power moves. I respected the girl's hustle and wanted to help her in any way I could. I just hoped my generosity didn't end up backfiring on me.

November 2006

*A*ll right, Si-Si, here's the deal: you gonna go in there and ask about his personal training program."

"What's his name?" Si-Si interrupted.

"You're going to know who he is because when you first walk in it's going to be quiet," I explained. "Then you're going to notice a man get louder and louder. It'll be him. He'll notice you and try to get your attention. He loves showing off for pretty girls."

"O-kay," Si-Si said.

"Once you spot 'im, go near him and work out where he can see you and you can see him. Just when you see him getting ready to leave that's when you ask 'im about training you. He gonna run down some prices and you gonna run down some game. Tell 'im you just got out here and you're tryna to get on your feet. Let 'im know that you were told that you had to lose a couple pounds and get fit before you could sign with an agent. Tell 'im that ya grandmom is sick and her wellness depends on your ability to support her and that's why you're so desperate to get work. I'm tellin' you, he'll bite. He's a typical captain save-a-ho." I paused and clarified, "Not that you're a ho and you need savin'. Well, let's be real. You are a ho and you do need savin'."

Si-Si laughed as she stepped out of my car.

"I'm serious," I told her.

"I know, I know," she said, wiping the smile off her face.

"Wherever you end up, catch a cab back to your house. Call me when you're on your way and I'll meet you there."

Si-Si nodded and with much sass trotted toward the door of L.A.'s most exclusive gym. I felt like a proud mom, watching her go forth with so much confidence.

I drove out of the gym's parking lot and decided to call Sean and see if we could get together. Thinking about Si-Si possibly gettin' with Corey put me in the mood to be up under a nigga. Plus, I wanted to arrange a meeting between Sean and Si-Si. I didn't plan to sic her on him like I had done with Corey. I mean, I myself was still fuckin' Sean so having her seduce him was out of the question. I just wanted them to meet with hopes of him seeing some potential in her and maybe throwing some work her way. But Corey, he and I stopped dealing with each other more than two weeks ago after he found out that Sean and I were an item. So having Si-Si make him a friend with benefits didn't matter to me at all.

"Hey sexy," I said after hearing Sean's voice say hello.

"What's up?" he replied, sounding all glad I called and shit.

"Whatchu doin'?"

"Stuck in traffic," he complained.

"Are you going or coming?" I asked.

"Going," he answered. "On my way to the office."

"Don't you just wish you were coming instead?" I flirted some more.

Sean chuckled. "Hell yeah," he said.

"Well, that's one thing we have in common this morning."

"Where are you?"

"I just left the gym."

"Corey's?" he asked, jealousy in his tone.

"No! I told you I don't train with him no more. Now, can we continue our phone sex before you turn me off?" I huffed.

"All right. Where were we?"

"I was saying how we both would rather be coming right now."

"Yeah, that's right. So, where would you be coming?"

"Umm"—I thought about it—"on your lips. What about you?"

"Your ass."

"How about my titties? They miss you so much," I suggested.

"I'm thinkin' more like ya pussy," Sean said.

"That's already flooded," I told him.

"Oh yeah? Who beat me to it?"

"Pointer and middle."

"Who the fuck are they?" Sean asked, confused.

"My fingers." I chuckled. "They got my pussy so wet you can swim in it."

Sean broke down and said roughly, "Meet me at my office."

"I thought you'd never ask," I told him. "I'll see you there."

I made my way over to Sean's Beverly Hills office. It took me less than a half hour, which was good for that time of the morning. Sean had gotten there a couple minutes before me and greeted me in the lobby of the building. We kissed each other gently in the presence of the security guards and by-standers in the lobby. But once we stepped on the elevator and the doors closed, we started fucking each other with our clothes on. We were fondling each other like crazy. Sean was sucking on my neck and I was caressing his balls. The minute the elevator stopped at our floor we straightened up. The doors opened and to the people who were waiting to get on, we looked like two strangers who happened to be getting off the elevator on the same floor. And in that short time period, my body was itching for more of Sean. I couldn't wait to pick up where we left off. We went into his office and he cleared his desk. Then Sean and I fucked like rabbits, trying to conceal our moans so that his colleagues wouldn't be alarmed.

I ended up staying at Sean's office with him the whole day. I played games on his computer, checked my e-mail, and browsed gucci.com to see what I could get Sean to buy me for my earlier services. I didn't see anything that was striking, so I let him slide. After the damn near ten hours we spent at Sean's office, we went out to dinner. Before then, though, we went to buy me something to wear. I had on sweats, seeing as how my plan for that day was to drop Si-Si off and go back home. I had no idea I would wind up at Ruth's Chris'.

During dinner, Sean got a phone call from one of his colleagues, an up-and-coming director who had just landed a major production deal for a film he wanted to make. Apparently, the guy wanted to bring Sean on board as a producer and in the midst of the conversation, I heard Sean tell him that he might have the perfect girl for one of the roles. I didn't know who Sean was referring to until after he hung up with the guy and told me in a couple of weeks I should expect a call from a casting director for a film titled *Gun Play*. Sean then nonchalantly continued chewing his filet mignon as if what he had just told me was no big deal. I didn't scream and shout like I wanted to. It just wasn't the time or the place, but I did crack an elaborate smile. I felt myself getting wet as I watched Sean cockily eat. That damn man was a hell of a turn-on and the way he looked out for me was granted to give him unlimited access to my goods.

I spent the night at Sean's loft and left when he did in the morning. I drove to my condo in the early rush-hour traffic, which was a huge mistake, and by the time I got home I was ready to go back to bed. I thought about Si-Si and wondered why she hadn't called me to tell me how things went with her and Corey. I worried briefly at the thought of not hearing from her. But I figured no news was good news and wrote off any concern. I traded my sweats for a nightshirt and slid in between my cozy white sheets and fluffy comforter from the Hotel Collection. I calmed myself catching the end of *Live with Regis and Kelly* but fell asleep before the commercials ended.

It was close to one o'clock in the afternoon when Si-Si called, waking me up to tell me that she was on her way home.

"Um, excuse me, it's a whole different day from when I dropped you off and told you to call me. Where the hell have you been?" I sounded off, my voice raspy. "For a minute I thought the nigga kidnapped you."

The breath Si-Si took before she spoke sounded giddy, so I just knew I was in for a love story. I turned over on my back and reclined against two pillows. Wiping my eyes, I tuned in to hear Si-Si tell all.

"Oh my God, girl, you did not tell me that he was workin' with that kind of power!" she screamed.

I instantly got a visual of Corey's jumbo manhood and I was wide awake. "Ya whore ass didn't give me time! I didn't think it would go down the same day you met 'im. I was thinkin' y'all would schedule the damn sessions first!"

"Well, it doesn't matter. It was a pleasant surprise! The nigga is huuuuge!" she squealed.

Stuck on stupid, I asked, "So what? Y'all fucked right there in the gym?"

"Not quite," Si-Si began. "I sucked him off in the bathroom, then he asked me—"

"You dirty little bitch!" I joked, interrupting Si-Si. "Let me find out I met my match. So go 'head, continue."

Si-Si chuckled. "So then he asked me to leave with him . . ."

"He took you to his personal gym?"

"No. To his house."

"His house? Where he live at? What it look like?"

"He got a big-ass house in Beverly Hills. Girl, laid out too. He's definitely gettin' it."

"Oh my God. I don't believe this shit! You must be good at what you do!"

"I told you this is what I do best! It's a lot you don't know about me," Si-Si bragged.

"For somebody who don't wanna play or even like to play the game, you sure sound content," I said, trying to get up in Si-Si's head and make sure her words could be taken at face value.

"Right now it's not about what I wanna do or what I like to

do. It's about me making money and putting myself in position to do bigger and better things. Shit, my grandmom is losing her health and if I gotta fuck a few niggas to get her taken care of, then that's what I'm gonna do, whether I like it or not," Si-Si stated.

"I feel you," I said, satisfied with her answer. I got back on subject. "Well I guess there's no need for me to ask you if Corey agreed to train you, huh?"

"Train me? Child, please. The nigga invited me to be his date at Johnny Depp's masquerade party next week!"

"What masquerade party? I ain't heard nothing about that."

"He just put out the invites today. The *Pirates* DVD set a sales record over in the UK, so he's doing a theme party to celebrate that plus the release of the DVD here in the States."

"That's gonna be the move, Si-Si. Johnny Depp? You know how many connections you can make in that one night?"

"You mean how many connections *we* can make," Si-Si corrected me.

"I ain't get no invitation," I whined.

"Yeah, but you know Sean gonna get one and who the fuck else would he take if not you?"

"Yeah, you right," I agreed. "I'll slit a nigga's throat."

"Exactly," Si-Si played along.

"That's gonna put us right where we need to be!" I told her, thinking of all the power players that would likely be present.

"Oh, I'm already on it. And believe me when I tell you, I know how to work a room."

"I know that's right," I told Si-Si. "We need to go shopping!" I blurted out.

"I know. We gotta find us the hottest pirate-type costumes in the city."

"We might have to get something made," I thought aloud.

"It gotta be sexy, but classy."

"It gotta be different too. We can't come in there lookin' like every other bitch."

"What's a sexy, unique costume from that movie?"

"Beats me. Shit, we need to watch the movie."

"Go rent it and meet me at my house," Si-Si said.

"It ain't out yet, fool," I reminded her.

"Oh yeah, that's right. Well, you wanna go to the movies?"

"It's probably not in the theaters no more if it's about to come out on DVD," I pointed out.

"You right."

"Bootleg," we both said as if we were reading each other's minds.

"We'll get the real one when it comes out," I said. Indirectly, I was justifying our decision to go against the code of ethics in our very own field.

"Yeah, of course," Si-Si cosigned.

Si-Si and I watched *Pirates of the Caribbean: Dead Man's Chest* at her house. Her mom and her grandmom watched it with us. We had a big bowl of popcorn, sodas, and candy like we were at the movies. We were all into it too. I never realized just how good that movie was. Johnny Depp played the hell out of his role. I couldn't wait to meet him at his party.

December 2006

After finally getting off Route 101 and making our way to Hollywood Boulevard and Highland Avenue, Sean and I could see the bright lights and exotic cars outside of Montmartre Lounge. The red carpet was cluttered with photographers snapping away at the attendees. Sean pulled his Maserati to the curb and a valet rushed over. The guy assisted me out of the passenger side and then tended to Sean. Sean tipped the guy and instructed him to leave his car up front. I was on the sidewalk watching Sean walk over to me, laughing internally at how funny he looked in his costume. He was dressed as a swash-buckler pirate, whatever that was. All I knew was that he looked like a black slave-owner with a patch over his eye. Somehow he was still sexy, though.

We reached the carpet and the cameras got to flickering. Sean had me on his arm, shamelessly showing me off to every lens. I enjoyed the attention, of course. Once inside the sleek club, Sean and I made our way through the celebrities and high rollers, stopping every couple feet to greet someone Sean knew, from Kate Hudson to Orlando Bloom. It was hard for me to tell who was who with all the eye patches, masks, and wigs, but I figured I'd flirt with every nigga in there. The chances of him being somebody were very high.

After Sean and I showed our faces to the entire club, we ended up upstairs where the *Pirates* movie was playing on a roll-down screen. Apparently Johnny Depp hadn't arrived yet, but I noticed that Si-Si had—and when she said she knew how to work a room she wasn't lying. Poor Corey was sitting at the bar sipping what looked to be vodka, and my girl Si-Si was across the room having a good ol' time with somebody dressed like Captain Hook.

"Sean, I'll be right back," I said, getting up off the plush couch we had been sitting on, engaging in small talk with Tom Hollander, the English actor who played Lord Cutler Beckett in *Pirates*.

I walked over to Si-Si and excused myself for cutting in on her and Captain Hook's conversation.

"Si-Si?" I asked, as if I didn't know her.

"Celess," she sang as if it was her first time seeing me in years.

We hugged and kissed each other on the cheek. Then Si-Si introduced me to her chat buddy.

"Celess, this is Christopher Walken. Chris, this is a friend of mine, Celess."

I shook Christopher's hand and he pulled me in for a hug and kisses on my cheeks. He was obviously tipsy and very cool and down to earth. I couldn't believe that damn Si-Si. I mean, the party had only been going on for an hour, and she was already drinking and laughing with the King of New York.

I complimented Si-Si on her costume: a white crop top that fell off her shoulders and showed just enough cleavage, accented with a red band that snugged up right under her breasts. The sleeves were puffy. And on her bottom was a full-length black skirt with a red mock belt. Her sandy blond and chocolate brown hair was separated down the middle, and she wore a red bandana over it.

Si-Si returned the compliment, especially expressing interest in my dress, a black leather lace-up corset top with red ties and a short flared red-and-white checkered skirt with black lace lining the bottom. It barely reached the middle of my thighs. My hair was up in an *I Dream of Jeannie* ponytail, and I had tied a red bandana around it. I had on a pair of black fishnet stockings and some knee-high black boots.

We both looked like sexy pirate wenches, and we were so glad we didn't opt for that damn *Elizabeth* costume. So many chicks had on that white princess-looking dress, you would have thought we were at one of Diddy's white parties. *The feel-*

ing you feel when you're dressed like another bitch at a party is sickening, I thought. Anyway, I let Si-Si continue on with Christopher fuckin' Walken and decided to help myself to the open bar.

I was standing near the bar, sipping my Krug Rosé and finally getting a chance to observe my surroundings. The Caribbean decor was cute. The glass tables were held up by treasure chests, and the centerpieces were vases filled with seashells, gold coins, and ocean-blue water. Headlines about the movie breaking sales records and being a box-office success were projected onto the floor. All the waitresses were dressed in burgundy corseted vests with white mock sleeves and burgundy pants that resembled gauchos. The waiters were in black-and-white striped pants, white button-down shirts, black vests, red sashes, and red bandanas. And all that was being served was seafood. It was a well-put-together party.

I had just taken a lobster brochette off the tray of complimentary hors d'oeuvres when someone crept up on me from behind. I turned around to see Corey's drunken ass trying to kiss me on my neck.

"Where you been?" he asked in my ear.

I stepped out of his arms and faced him. "I been around. Are you all right?" I asked, frowning slightly.

"Yeah," he said, smiling to reveal a fake gold tooth, one of the night's popular pirate accessories. "I just ain't seen you in a while."

"Yeah, well I've been very busy, that's all." I bit my brochette and sipped my champagne. "You here alone?"

Corey twisted his drunken lips and said, "I might as well be. The chick I came with just upped and left me sitting at the bar to babysit her drink."

"Um," I said, pretending I didn't know the story already. Si-Si and I agreed that we wouldn't let it be known that we were friends. We figured it would raise red flags to Corey and Sean if they knew how tight we were. Corey would know we were running game on him, and Sean would feel insecure about me letting my best friend mess with my ex. He would swear it was my way of still being in touch with him or some shit. So we planned to keep our distance from each other at the party and make it look like we were only associates.

"What about you?" Corey asked. "Where's your date?"

"He's over there watching the movie," I told him.

"Why you ain't over there with 'im then?"

"I already saw it."

Just then, all the lights dimmed down close to dark. One of the songs from the movie blasted through the sound system. Parting the crowd were these two big muscular men carrying a big wooden chair. In it was Johnny Depp, dressed elaborately as Captain Jack Sparrow in the scene where he became a native god to the Pelegostos. The crowd of attendees cheered and clapped at Johnny Depp's grand entrance. I myself didn't budge. I stood stiff, admiring the man. Never before had I looked at him in such a way. I mean, he was the shit in *Blow*, but it wasn't until seeing him in that damn Jack Sparrow wardrobe that I fell in love with him. I didn't know if it was that dark eyeliner or the weird-ass expression on his face that drew me in. But I was on him like lightning on a rod. I quickly requested another glass of Krug and the next thing I knew, I was walking over to him in front of the entire party.

He hadn't even gotten out of the chair yet, which was the perfect time to approach him. I stood in front of him holding two glasses of champagne. I handed him one and clinked my glass against his.

"Toast to a job well done," I said, taking a sip.

He put up his glass to accept my toast and he sipped his champagne. We eyed each other briefly, and then I fell back into the crowd. Everybody cheered again, and Johnny Depp got up to walk around and greet his guests.

I felt so empowered that I was convinced he would seek me out before the night was over. Si-Si walked over to me and winked.

"You are one crazy bitch," she said, seemingly half drunk.

"Did I kill it or did I kill it?" I asked slyly.

"You killed it," she confirmed. Then looking past me, she said, "Here he comes."

I exhaled slowly as Johnny Depp's voice penetrated my eardrums.

"So what's the mysterious woman's name?" he asked.

I turned around and smiled. "Celess. And yours?"

He wrinkled his face as if to say, *You don't know?*

"Well, it's one of two names," I said, explaining myself. "Johnny or Jack?"

He smiled and said, "Tonight, it's Jack."

I nodded and extended my hand. "Pleased to meet you."

"Same here. Thanks for the drink, by the way."

"Don't mention it. It's on the house." I smiled.

Johnny smiled along with me, and before he got whisked away by Bill Nighy he made me promise him a dance before I left. I did and then decided to find Sean and kick it with him in the meantime.

"Hey baby," I said, walking up to Sean and kissing him on his lips.

"You havin' a good time?" he asked, eyes glassy.

I nodded my head.

"I saw you go over there and toast Johnny. That was cute." He laughed.

"He did such an amazing job in the film, plus I'm tipsy as all hell," I explained.

"Hey, he deserved it," Sean agreed. "You need to follow up on that."

"What do you mean?" I asked.

"He's a hell of a contact," he elaborated. "That's what this business is about . . . making contacts."

"Well, he did ask if he could have one dance before I left,"

I revealed. "But I didn't wanna make you feel uncomfortable."

Sean frowned and said, "Do ya thing. It's all good."

Getting the green light from Sean was all I needed to act a fool. I had a couple more drinks and loosened up completely. People were approaching me wanting to know who I was after I pulled that stunt on Johnny. Men and women were introducing themselves. They all thought I was somebody big. When it was all said and done, I got a dance in with Johnny Depp and stored his number in my Dash. The whole party knew me as Celess, Shiner's newest supermodel, and I collected so many business cards and accepted dances with so many fine Hollywood actors, you would have thought I was already an A-lister.

Si-Si and I made out like bandits at the *Pirates* party and started getting gigs left and right. A jeweler from Palisades approached Si-Si about being the face for his new line. She did a photo shoot for him in Marina del Rey, and one of the shots became a billboard in the jewelry district in downtown L.A. She took her mom and grandmom down there to see it and her mom almost fainted. It was so funny.

That same photo was published in just about every high-end magazine from *Vogue* to *W*. Si-Si was also the hostess at the reveal party for the jewelry line, and it was there that she met video director Benny Boom. He told her that he had some projects in the works that she would be perfect for and invited her out to New York for Nas' album release party.

"Shit, I got an audition on that Tuesday morning." I shot down Si-Si's exciting news about us flying to New York.

"Audition for what?" Si-Si asked, perturbed.

"That movie *Gun Play* Sean hooked me up with. No way I'll be able to hang out all night in New York on Monday and be at the audition in L.A. at ten in the morning Tuesday."

Si-Si was quiet for a minute. I assumed she was thinking up a plan.

"You can always get on a red-eye right after the party," she suggested.

"And show up to my audition in a minidress reeking of Patrón?"

"Girl, pack you a pair of sweats and plenty mints, spray on some J'adore, and keep it movin'!"

"I don't know. I mean, an audition for a movie, which can make me famous, or a fuckin' album release party, which can only make me seen." I lifted my hands as if they were scales, weighing my options. "Audition!"

"Or *both*!" Si-Si exclaimed. "You never know what can come out of the party. That's a whole new world, New York. And shit, that's movie central over there. You might fuck around and see Spike Lee in that bitch."

"It is where I got my start," I reflected. "I might run into some old faces and get put on some next-level shit."

"I'll book our flights." Si-Si jumped to conclusions.

I sighed and said, "All right, got damnit. But if I fuck up on my audition, you gonna owe me the money I woulda made off that mothafuckin' movie."

Si-Si reached across the table and hugged me, almost knocking over my latte. We were in Starbucks off Beverly Glen Boulevard. Si-Si was on her laptop typing her résumé. I was doing a crossword puzzle. The both of us were recuperating from the night before, which we spent at Terry and Derrek's fiftieth birthday dinner party at a beautiful mansion in Paradise Valley, Arizona.

We listened to a live band, drank, and exchanged compliments and gossip with men aged forty and up and women aged eighteen to twenty-five. It was the most boring party ever until this young muscular male stripper came walking in carrying a five-tier cake singing, "Happy birthday, Celess." I was surprised that Derrek and Terry remembered my birthday let alone allowed me to celebrate with them. The real shock came when I was directed outside to the driveway and there was a seafrost Jaguar XK convertible with a big red bow around it. Derrek handed me the key and his exact words to me were: "You're my wife's sister. Plus, you're living out in L.A. now. I can't have you riding around in a three series." I was in awe.

After that the party began. A DJ replaced the band, the lights dimmed, and everybody was up on their feet shaking their asses and bopping their heads. Si-Si was having a ball, flirting with all the older wealthy men. That was definitely her crowd. She knew just how to rub them old-ass white men the right way. I even walked up on her talking to one guy in Italian. And I'm not talking a simple hello. They were having a full-blown conversation. I made a mental note to ask her about the hidden talent. I mean, I knew she spoke Spanish because that was how she communicated with her mom and grandmom all the time. But there weren't any Italian mother-fuckas in her family that I knew of.

After making her rounds, Si-Si asked if I could put her on Derrek, noticing how deep his pockets were, but I let her know that he was one man who was off limits to her. Derrek was my girl Tina's man whether she was here or not. And if it was up to me he wouldn't mess with another chick ever. Si-Si understood and moved on to the next filthy rich man with sugar daddy potential.

I just watched her in admiration. There was something about that girl that was deeper than the eye could see. She had some secrets of her own, I was sure, and I would make it my business to find out what they were. But at that time I just continued watching her enviously, living through her that night, thinking about how smart of her it was to bring her jewelry beau as her date. She was able to waltz in with a mil-lionaire on her arm, keep her business relationship with him fresh, and still have the freedom to romance other big-pocket men at the party. Of course I took Sean. It was just like me to be tied up with a nigga and wind up being seen with him everywhere. I mean, don't get me wrong, I liked Sean a lot and he was definitely a key to my success, but I didn't feel as free as I wanted to be with him around. Yeah, he encouraged me to network while I was out with him, but what if I wanted to take my networking to my bedroom? That wasn't happening as long as he was by my side. And that was the part I was beginning to miss.

I did know one thing, though: in New York, at the *Hip Hop Is Dead* release party, I would make up for lost time.

It was freezing on the East Coast and Si-Si and I couldn't wait to get inside the Capitale on the Lower East Side of New York. We were outside waiting for the line of people to adorn the black carpet, walk up the steps, and pour inside when a hearse pulled up in front of the grand building, causing a scene. Everyone turned to see who the hell would come to Nas' party in a damn hearse and lo and behold, it was Nas his damn self. He stepped out of the funeral prop with his wife, Kelis, and the crowd oohhed and ahhhed. We all got the joke at that point. *Hip-hop is dead—a hearse.* It was cute, and it made me think about Johnny Depp's themed entrance weeks ago and how I couldn't wait to be famous enough to throw such lavish parties.

Flashes from the numerous cameras lit up the front door as Nas and Kelis were escorted into the club. Si-Si told me she grabbed Nas' hand and rubbed it as he brushed by her. I laughed at her and told her she wasn't shit. We were already tipsy from indulging in happy hour cocktails at our hotel earlier. So we were bound to behave badly once we really started to party. I was definitely up for it. It had been a while since I was out without Sean, not to mention I was miles away from him. I had every intention of acting a fool.

Among the stars at Nas' party were Mark Wahlberg, Omarion, and—like Si-Si guessed—Spike Lee, but it was Jay-Z and Beyoncé I was most happy to meet. They were the hottest couple in the business and both of them were at the top of their game. They were paid out the ass and you couldn't do shit but love 'em for it. Shit, I was tryin' to be just like 'em.

We took pictures with just about everybody and the funny thing was, people were asking *us* to take pictures with *them*. It wasn't like we were going up to mothafuckas being all joe and shit. It all started when a cameraman asked me and Si-Si to pose near the casket that was against a wall in the extravagant club. He must have taken twenty pictures of us and we were posing too, like we were shooting for magazines or some shit. People started to notice and came walking over to us asking to be in our pictures. We didn't mind; shit, it was a good look. The next thing we knew we were immersed in conversations with very big names. The goal from there was to go back to a hotel suite with one of them paid mothafuckas, and that we did.

Si-Si and I ended our night at the Waldorf Towers. Drunk as hell off of countless shots of Patrón, we participated in an orgy with two of the music industry's highest-paid performers. I didn't show up at the airport for my red-eye flight back out to California because my new dude chartered me and Si-Si a private jet to take us home. We got to L.A. at seven in the morning. I ended up showering and changing my clothes at Si-Si's apartment. She drove me to my audition, stopping at Starbucks to grab two coffees on the way. We were quiet the whole car ride, I guess thinking about the wild night before. For me, I was also thinking about getting the audition over and done with so I could get home and go to bed.

The audition was packed with women in my age group with similar physical characteristics. And many of them could really act. I was sure that this would be one role I wouldn't get. I was tired as shit and recovering from a hangover, plus I wasn't a trained actress like many of the women were. But hell, I was there bright and early after just landing a few hours ago so I might as well do what I came to do. I was sitting out in the hall waiting for my name to be called. A short dark-skinned guy walked past me and the other women who were waiting. A short while later, he reappeared and instead of walking past, he stopped in front of us.

"Which one of you is Celess?" he asked us.

"I am," I said.

"Follow me," he said.

I stood up and walked behind the guy. I felt like a giant compared to him—he couldn't be taller than five feet. He walked into an office and I followed behind him. He closed the door.

"Hey Celess," he said reaching out his short stubby hand. "I'm Arren."

"Nice to meet you," I said, shaking his hand. I didn't know who he was even after he told me his name. Sean's friend who had hooked me up with the audition was named Jay so "Arren" didn't ring any bells.

"I'm the one who scheduled your appointment this morning," he began to explain. "I work with the casting agency."

"Oh, okay, I spoke with you on the phone a little while back," I remembered.

"Right, right. So I hear you're good friends with Sean Harrison."

"Yeah. We're cool." I played down Sean's and my relationship.

"Yeah." He nodded. "Well, I guess we better get started before somebody comes wandering in here."

I looked around the empty and quiet office and wondered what Arren meant. But before I could ask, he started unbuckling his belt.

"You'll get the part," he said, taking down his pants. "I can guarantee you that."

Aw, what the fuck, I thought. *I gotta suck this dwarf's dick*

*for this damn role? That's some bullshit! And how was I to know
that he was the real deal? Shit, he isn't Jay. I could see if he was
Jay. I would have sucked him off quick with no reservations. But
this nigga is just the appointment scheduler. He's like a fuckin'
secretary. Why the fuck am I about to suck his little-ass dick?* I
was burned up, but I assumed the position. Hell, if he turned
out to be a fraud, I would just have to suck it up as I took one
for the team.

Christmas rolled around and the best gift I received was the
lead role in *Gun Play*. Si-Si and I celebrated to no end. I had
gotten my first lead in a major production and since the ren-
dezvous in New York she and I both had become starlets.
Si-Si had been getting a lot of modeling gigs and had been
endorsing everything from perfume to exotic cars. Me, on the
other hand? I'd been getting music video gigs and acting gigs,
including a recurring role on a popular HBO series. We were
up with both fame and fortune. And it seemed that we had
snuck in Hollywood's back door and became overnight celebrities. It was the holiday season and things were going great so
it was bottle-poppin' every night for a whole week. Then we
topped it off with a New Year's Eve party at Tao nightclub in
Vegas hosted by Pamela Anderson.

"Three . . . two . . . one—Happy New Year's!" everybody
shouted as the clock struck midnight.

I took a gulp of my champagne straight from the bottle as

I looked around at all the people. It was as if everything was in slow motion. People were laughing, drinking, smiling, and partying, having a ball, living it up. They all seemed so happy, including Si-Si, who was taking her bottle of champagne to the head as well. Sean was behind me holding my waist and Si-Si's latest boy toy, actor David Cunningham, was beside him. I was so drunk my head felt light and I struggled to keep my eyes open. Usually under such influence I felt good as shit, happy and carefree. But that night was different. I was so sad that I burst into tears.

"What's wrong?" Si-Si shouted over the loudness. Her happy face turned into one of concern.

I shook my head as if to say nothing and wiped my eyes, trying to hold back the tears.

Si-Si reached out and grabbed my arm, pulling me away from Sean.

"We're going to the bathroom," she told him.

She guided my wobbly ass to the bathroom, held me up against the sink, and looked me in my teary eyes.

"What's wrong?" she asked me again. "Why are you crying?"

I wasn't going to say anything at first, but I felt like I needed to vent.

"This exact date five years ago I saw my best friend get shot to death," I cried. "And I got shot in my face at close range."

"*Whaaat?*" Si-Si asked, surprised. "Who the hell did that?"

I shook my head and responded, "Some dude we pissed off." I kept it vague, not wanting to reveal my secret to Si-Si. Then I went on, "It feels like just yesterday that shit happened. Like my best friend was just here kickin' it with me and now she's gone and I miss her so much," I wept.

You know what, bitch? You fucked with the wrong one! POP! POP! Flashbacks of that night played in my head as I cried in Si-Si's arms.

"Damn, I'm so sorry to hear that." Si-Si tried consoling me. "Believe me, I feel your pain," she said, sniffling.

"I feel so guilty that I lived. I mean, why didn't I just die with her?"

Si-Si took her arms from around me and stepped back so that she could look at me while she spoke. "God wasn't ready for you. It wasn't your time and there's nothing you can do about that."

"I just wish she was here, that's all. She's the one who put me on my feet and I just wish she could be here to share all this with me, you know."

"I know," Si-Si said. "But you know what? If she put you on your feet then that means she was a good person, and therefore she's probably up there cheering you on. She don't want you to feel guilty for shit. And I bet you she hopin' you dry your tears and go back out there and pop a bottle for her."

I chuckled at the thought of hearing Tina's voice saying, "Girl, wipe your eyes." Si-Si was right. Tina was probably up in heaven rooting for me. I wiped my tears and touched up my makeup. Si-Si and I left the bathroom and I went straight to the bar. I ordered a bottle of Moët for old times' sake and held it up to the ceiling. *This one's for you, Tina,* I thought as I popped open the bottle and drank myself dizzy.

At the night's end, I was carried out of the club by Sean. "Happy New Year's, mothafuckas! It's been one hell of a year!" was the last I remember saying before passing out.

January 2007

*C*eless, Si-Si!" "Celess, Si-Si!" I never thought the day would come when paparazzi and the media would be screaming my name for a photo op. But there I was, walking the red carpet at the People's Choice Awards at the Shrine Auditorium in L.A. and my name being shouted from every direction. A couple of pictures here, a few brief interviews there—it was crazy. I participated, though, being nice and stopping for everybody. I got some plugs in about my first lead role coming up and I even announced an address where I could receive fan mail. Things were going smoothly at first.

Si-Si and I were posing for every photographer to the point that my lips started quivering from smiling so much. I took a brief moment to exercise my mouth muscles and as I was doing so a loud voice called out, "Is that how you solidified your spot in Hollywood?"

I couldn't tell who the voice belonged to, although it

sounded like Wendy Williams, a loudmouthed radio personality in New York who was known for being a gossip queen. But I didn't know for sure and it was a good thing too, because Si-Si and I would have embarrassed ourselves beating down that bitch. I just ignored the comment and kept it movin'. Si-Si did the same. Too bad the reporters didn't. They must have felt liberated because right after the first ignorant question followed a host of others.

"Is it true that you're dating David Cunningham?" a voice called out to Si-Si.

"Is it true you had sex with the casting director to get your upcoming role in *Gun Play*?"

"Who are you dating this month, Si-Si?"

"Celess, are you and Sean Harrison sharing Si-Si?"

The questions were coming out of left field. I can't say that I was surprised because the paparazzi were always all in your business. But damn, all those disrespectful questions on the red carpet? How fuckin' low could they go? I was so ready to bring Philly out on their asses and knock 'em in the fuckin' mouth. But I chilled off the strength of maintaining my position that I had worked so hard to get. Besides, I wasn't the first celebrity the paparazzi harassed and I wasn't going to be the last. It was their job to dig up dirt on people, so hell, I let it go.

Si-Si and I were so happy to be inside the Shrine it didn't make any sense. We were relieved we got through the humiliation parade without losing our cool. Once inside, we became uplifted, reveling in the fact that we had made it in the business. Regardless of what we did to get here, we were *here* and that was all that was important. We sat down in our seats, which were next to our superstar friend Johnny Depp and his peoples.

"Good to see you again," I told him, kissing him on his cheek.

Si-Si greeted him as well and then we both greeted his small entourage. I wished him luck before the show began and he thanked me. As bad as I wanted to fuck that man, I didn't allow myself to go there with him. I respected his relationship. Plus, we were friends, and shit, it was our friendship that got me and Si-Si those seats so I didn't want to do anything to mess that up. But that sure didn't stop me from fantasizing about him the whole awards show, though. A couple of times I was tempted to touch myself, I was so horny. But I didn't. I was sitting next to one of the number one nominees so the camera would be on me sporadically throughout the evening. It would have been a mess had it caught me playing with my pussy. *Oh my goodness, I would be too through.* I smirked at my nasty and crazy thoughts and continued watching the show. Seeing my favorite movie stars up close and personal was the shit. But no one seemed to be more enamored than Si-Si. She was really living her dream, I could tell. And you couldn't tell the bitch nothing either.

Johnny Depp ended up winning like three awards. Other winners were Halle Berry, Jennifer Aniston, and Justin Timberlake. As the show ended and people scattered to their cars, I was approached by one sexy-ass white man.

He asked me if I was going to stay for the after party. I told him only if he was.

He chuckled and said, "Celess, right?"

I nodded, figuring he had seen me on TV or read about me in a magazine somewhere. "And you are?" I asked, not recognizing him as anybody famous.

"Cliff," he said, "Cliff Warner."

"It's a pleasure to meet you," I said, taking note of his famous last name.

"The pleasure is all mine," he told me. "You are absolutely beautiful."

I wanted to say no shit, now take me to a hotel and fuck me hard 'cause Johnny Depp got my pussy wetter than the Pacific Ocean, but I didn't. I just thanked him and smiled.

I convinced Si-Si to stay at the party with me instead of going straight to hook up with David.

"Sean is in Vancouver shooting that foreign film and I do not want to spend another night alone," I reminded her. "Plus, you got all night to get with David. All I'm asking for is a few hours."

"My baby doesn't feel well," she whined. "Why can't you get this dude's number and hook up with him later?"

I decided to pour it on. "Si-Si, you have to work with me here. Not only is the man gorgeous, but he belongs to one of the wealthiest families in the business."

"Who is he?" Si-Si wanted confirmation.

"He's a Warner," I told her.

Her bottom lip dropped and she said, "Well in that case, do you. But is it possible you can book his ass within an hour because I don't wanna leave my baby waiting long."

"All right, cool."

I got Cliff nice and toasty and ended up spending the night with him at the Peninsula Beverly Hills. He wanted to take the party to my house, but I wasn't going to disrespect Sean to the degree of bringing another man into my bed. I wasn't that cutthroat.

In the morning, though, I realized that I should have done exactly that. At least then there wouldn't have been a million photographers outside to capture Cliff and me leaving together in the attire we had on the night before. I tried my damnedest to hide my face, but it didn't work.

In fact, that following Monday, Cliff and I were blasted on the front of *Us Weekly*. All types of stories ran about us, from us being one-night-standers to us being secretly married. I was hot—not so much at the stories because that was just hearsay, but about the pictures. I didn't want them to get back to Sean. There was no explanation for them. And Sean didn't deserve to be done wrong like that. Si-Si and I bought up all the issues we could find. We literally drove all over L.A. trying to confiscate the magazines.

Si-Si thought it was a good publicity stunt and said that if Sean ever did find out, that was what I should tell him. I thought it over; she had a point. People in the business staged photos all the time to get some press so it didn't sound far-fetched, I told myself. I figured I wouldn't stress over it any more than I already had, and whenever Sean confronted me about it I would simply tell him that it was staged. That was if he even found out. He was in another country for the next month or two so it was likely he would miss that issue anyway.

Who was I kidding? Celebrities never missed shit pertaining to other celebrities, let alone shit pertaining to themselves. Even if they didn't see it with their own eyes, somebody in their squad would and trust they were told all about it. Sean was no different. His publicist got ahold of the magazine and faxed the cover to his hotel in Vancouver.

"Celess, I been gone for seven fuckin' days and already you showin' ya ass!" Sean exploded at me.

I held my cell phone away from my ear to avoid going deaf from his shouting.

"Hello to you too," I said sarcastically.

"Now is not the time for jokes, seriously," he said. "Why the fuck are you on the cover of that magazine with this dude? What the fuck are you doin' out there?"

"Oh, that's what this is about?" I played it down. "That was just a damn photo op," I said, completely mixing up my terms.

"You and a nigga coming out of a hotel at ten o'clock in the morning is not a fuckin' photo op!" he shouted some more, sounding insulted that I would challenge his intelligence with a bullshit-ass lie.

By that time Si-Si was standing in front of me, whispering, "Not a photo op. A publicity stunt."

Shit, I thought, and then I got right back into it. "I meant a publicity stunt. Not a photo op. My bad."

"Oh, yeah? A publicity stunt? Who the fuck set that up and for what?" he demanded, seemingly not convinced.

"My agency set it up. They said it would be good press for my upcoming movie," I read off the napkin Si-Si was holding in front of my eyes.

"You ain't even start shooting that movie yet, Celess. But look, I'll holla at you. I gotta go."

Click.

I took a deep breath and rolled my eyes. *God damnit,* I thought.

"He ain't tryna hear that shit," I told Si-Si.

"Well, fuck it. You tried."

"But now I feel bad like shit," I confided.

"Yeah, me too. I liked Sean. He was my buddy."

"I know. He was good to me too."

"You better hope he don't blackball ya ass," Si-Si brought up.

"I know, right? Shit, I ain't think about that. That's all I need is to not get any more work." I was silent for a second and then I said, "I gotta find a way to get him to forgive me for this shit."

"You gonna have to spend some money on 'im," Si-Si suggested.

"What kind of money?" I asked.

"You better get 'im like a fuckin' Phantom or something."

"Bitch, you tryna empty my whole bank account."

"You act like you don't have friends in high places."

Catching on to what Si-Si was saying I asked, "So you saying I should hit Terry and Derrek up for several hundred thousand dollars to win back *my* man?"

"You better do something," Si-Si said.

"I ain't goin' that far," I said. "Suppose I ever need them for some serious shit? They gonna be like, get out of here, you still owe for that damn Phantom you bought for some nigga with *our* money."

"That money ain't gonna put a wrinkle in their pockets. They got it, trust. Plus, you can just tell 'em that the car is for you. Shit, you see he bought you a brand-new Jag without you even having to ask."

"I'm not in the business of abusing my power, especially not with people who really look out for me."

Si-Si huffed, "Well I don't know what to tell you."

"Why can't I just show up at his hotel naked underneath a trench coat?"

"That's old school. Niggas ain't fallin' for that shit anymore. Plus, he's pissed off at you so he gonna see right through that shit. Now, a hot wheel? A nigga gonna want that bitch so bad, he gonna be ready to marry ya ass for it."

I thought about what Si-Si was saying; the more I did the more I believed the girl was just crazy.

"Si-Si, I usually listen to you and your bright-ass ideas but this is one that just don't make no damn sense to me," I told her. "I'm not spending a half a mil on no nigga! I don't give a fuck who he is or what I did to him."

Si-Si nodded and said, "Well, let's just hope he don't turn the tables on ya ass."

Weeks went by without me hearing from Sean and I was miserable. I wanted my baby back. I felt so bad that I had hurt his feelings like that for the world to see. I wished I had brought that nigga Cliff to my house like he had suggested. Shit, by the time Sean got back I could have bought a new mattress set and acted like ain't shit happen. That would have been cheaper than the price I was paying for having been caught cheating.

I was sitting in the house bored and depressed, thinking about losing Sean. As much as I thought I wanted to be free, I didn't. Well, let me rephrase that—I didn't want to be alone. I decided to get out and get some fresh air before I got too caught up in my emotions. God knows that was a recipe for destruction.

I got off my couch, turned off my TV, and slid my feet into my Chanel sneakers. I went in the bathroom to touch up my makeup and fix my hair. I grabbed my black Chanel sunglasses out of my dressing room and threw them over my puffy eyes. I headed out the door, planning to stop by the post office and pick up my mail, maybe grab something to eat. Si-Si was spending the day in Beverly Hills with David so I couldn't get up with her. It was cool though because I really didn't feel like being bothered.

I could hardly open my post office box it was so cluttered with mail. I tugged on the tiny key until the door popped open. I grabbed the envelopes and stuffed them in my huge patent leather Chanel bag, then closed the box back and locked it. *Whose idea was it for me to start getting fan mail?* I thought. Proceeded out of the post office, pulled my sunglasses from atop my head and back over my eyes. The sun was beaming as it did most mornings, making the fifty degrees feel more like seventy. I got inside my Jaguar XK and drove toward downtown.

I returned to my condo at a little past four after first stopping and getting my dinner. As soon as I got in my house, I dropped my pocketbook and my keys on the sofa and went straight into the kitchen. I hadn't eaten anything all day and I was starving. Call me crazy, but I refused to be caught by the paparazzi eating something. Me in the midst of chewing was bound to produce an ugly photo. It wouldn't be a good look. So I made sure to be in the privacy of my own home whenever I planned to chow down.

I grabbed a bottled water from the refrigerator and put it on the counter while I transferred my chicken salad and two slices of gourmet pizza from Chinois on Main onto a paper plate. I sat down at my bar and said my grace. Then I tore the food up like it was my final meal.

"Mm, mm, mm," I mumbled, "I could kiss Wolfgang Puck."

I cleaned my plate, not leaving a single crumb, and went back into the kitchen to put the remainder of the food away. I drank the last of my water and walked into the living room, comfortably sinking into my sofa. My stomach was so full, it felt like it was going to burst. Instead of turning on the TV like I started to, I pulled the fan mail that had accumulated over just a couple weeks out of my pocketbook and placed the envelopes beside me.

I officially felt like a star as I opened my first letter. I read through it—it was pretty basic, stating how much I was loved by some guy in Minnesota. It was sweet. It made me blush. All of the letters to follow were just as basic. Some were from girls who loved my style or women who were aspiring to be actresses too. All in all, the mail wasn't that entertaining until I got to one letter in particular.

It was from a guy named Bernard Higgins who lived in Nebraska claiming that he knew me and had a relationship with me in the past back in Philly. Since Bernard wasn't sure who would be checking my mail—so he said—and didn't want his information to end up in the wrong hands, he didn't go into detail. However, he *did* include a telephone number and asked me to call him so that we could catch up. He congratulated me on my success and gave me a hint, saying that he was one of my exes.

I must have reread the letter a thousand times, trying to study the chicken scratch handwriting. Coming up with nothing, I beat my brains trying to recall a Bernard Higgins. I even ran down a list of possible nicknames in my head, like Bernie, Nard, B, but none of them rang any bells. I wanted to call the number and get to the bottom of the mystery man, but I was scared that it might be somebody I'd rather not reunite with. I decided to put the letter aside and go on to the next, although my curiosity bugged the shit out of me the whole time I read the other letters.

Finally, after about an hour, I decided to stop bitchin' and call Bernard's number. Who knew, it could have been a prank that I would be able to get some laughs out of, which I sure could use.

"Hello, can I speak to Bernard Higgins, please?" I was holding my cell up to my ear with my finger on the End button in case I needed to hang up quick.

"This is Bernard. Who's this?" the deep voice replied.

Although the voice sounded familiar, I couldn't pin it down.

"This is Celess," I said, slowly and hesitant.

"Celess." The voice grew upbeat. "It's me, O."

Then the voice made sense, but everything else didn't. O was dead. He was killed in a highway robbery. How the hell could he be on the other end of my phone?

"Who is this playing with me? And why?" I asked, half upset and half confused.

"I know this is hard for you to believe, but it is me. I didn't get killed. It was faked for my protection," the voice explained.

I pressed the End button and dropped my phone to the floor. Somebody was fucking with me and I didn't think it was cute. All I knew was they were dead wrong for pulling a prank like that. O meant a lot to me and when he got killed it messed me up.

Ring! Ring!

I picked up my phone and answered, "Cut it out for real, okay? This shit ain't funny at all!"

"Celess, I swear to you it's me. I'm not playing. I wouldn't do nothing—"

I interrupted the unknown caller. "O is dead! I saw the

fuckin' obituary!" Tears gathered in my eyes as I recalled O's face on the front of the threefold I had gotten from his aunt in Delaware some years back.

"All right, listen, I'll prove it to you. Then afterward I can explain everything."

"Whatever! Just don't call me again!" I hung up.

My phone was still in the palm of my hands when seconds later it alerted me to say that I'd received a picture message. I didn't know what to expect when I opened the message. But of everything, I damn sure didn't expect it to be a picture of O, alive and apparently well. I was in disbelief as I held the phone up to my eyes, examining it. Was I dreaming? What the hell was in that food I ate? I must have been poisoned because it was no way I was seeing what I thought I was seeing.

Ring! Ring!

"Hello," I answered, flustered. "What the hell is goin' on?"

"Celess, federal agents faked my death—I'm in a witness protection program. I go by Bernard Higgins now, but it's really me, O. I know this all sounds crazy as shit, but it's true. I shouldn't even be calling you and telling you this, but I couldn't help myself. I see you on TV now and you this big star and whatnot, and I be like damn I wish I could call her and just talk to her and let her know that I'm all right."

O went on and on as I listened in utter shock. And the more he talked the more familiar he sounded. It really *was* O. He *was* alive. I could have shit my pants I was so surprised.

"O? Are you fuckin' serious?" I broke my silence.

"It's crazy, I know, but it's me though."

"Oh my God! I don't believe this shit!"

"I wanna tell you everything but just not over the phone."

"Well where the fuck you at? I wanna see you!"

"You still got a dirty mouth, huh?" O chuckled.

"Nigga, because I'm trippin' over here right now talking to you! I don't believe it. This is bullshit! Who is fuckin' playin' these games with me?"

"What do I have to do to convince you that it's me? I already sent you a picture."

"I don't know," I said, still baffled. "Tell me something about me, something that only O would know."

"Um, let me see," O said. "You're a dude."

I threw my hand over my mouth and tears charged out of my eyes.

"Oh my God! Shut up!" I cried.

"I'm telling you. It's me," O pressed.

"O? You are fuckin' alive?"

"Yeah, I'm tryna tell you," he said. "So what's good with you?"

"What do you mean what's good with me? You can't just pop up after five years of me thinking you were killed and ask what's good with me!"

O laughed. "You still the same ol' Celess."

"I have to see you," I blurted out. "Where are you? I'll book a flight tonight!"

"I'm in Omaha, Nebraska," O said.

"Oma who?" I asked, rushing around my house looking for a pen to write the information down.

"Omaha," O enunciated.

"Why don't you come to L.A.?" I asked, having a change of heart about going all the way out to no-man's-land to see some guy I used to mess with who was supposed to be dead. Reality kicked in and I wondered if I was being set up.

"I can't," he said. "For protection purposes."

"Ain't nobody thinkin' 'bout you in L.A.! You'll be safe out here."

"Naw, but you a superstar now. I'm seen with you and next thing you know my face all over the TV and shit. That'll blow my whole spot," he said.

"So you saying you want me to come all the way out to some Omaha, Nebraska?" I asked, overly excited that I was talking to somebody I had so much love for.

"It ain't that far from where you at. I wanna see you, in person, not on no damn TV screen."

"I wanna see you too. Oh my God, I'm trippin'."

"Look, just book a flight out here."

I put aside my fear and asked, "Well, when do you want me to come out there?"

"Whenever," he said. "Whenever is convenient for you."

"Well, the sooner the better," I said trying to visualize

my calendar in my head. "I go away to shoot a movie in April . . ." I thought aloud.

O cut me off. "April? I'm talkin' about seeing you way before April. I'm talkin' 'bout like a week or so from now."

"But the Grammys," I whined.

"When are they?"

"February eleventh, I think," I told him.

"Well, come out here the first week of February. Then you could be back in time for the Grammys," he said patiently.

"You talkin' about me flyin' out in a couple of days, then."

"Yeah. Why not?"

I huffed as I thought about O's request. It would be nice to see him after so many years. But shit, he wasn't giving me time to prepare. On the other hand, it would be best to go see him before Sean came back to town. Even though we would probably be on the outs with each other, I didn't want to add salt to the wound by going away to spend a week with another nigga the minute he came back.

"I guess I can swing that," I gave in.

"Let me give you all my information," he said.

After setting up a reunion with O, I stayed on the phone with him into the next day, laughing, crying, and filling him in on what I'd been through over the years. Neither of us wanted to hang up. At least, I know I didn't. I think it was partly for fear that I would lose him again. It was like I was dreaming, and I didn't want to wake up. *O is alive. I'll be damned!*

February 2007

Because it was so last-minute, I couldn't get a nonstop flight to Omaha so I had a connection in Denver. I hated having to change planes. I thought it was the worst thing ever. Whoever thought of that shit should be shot. I had to leave the comfort of my first-class seat and then scramble through Denver's airport to my new gate, wait for the plane to board, and start from scratch getting comfortable in my new first-class seat. It was truly a pain in the ass.

The only benefit was that people recognized me and so I got special treatment. Airport security lugged my carry-on bags for me from gate to gate and I was first to board each flight.

When I arrived in Omaha it was dark outside. *Surprising for four in the afternoon,* I thought, looking at my watch. Then the captain spoke, and I realized that there was a two-hour time difference between L.A. and Omaha. It was actually six in the evening. Omaha's airport was as I expected it to be, small and lacking pizzazz. People were staring at me as I strutted to baggage claim. A few even asked me to take pictures with them. And to think, I'd dressed down to avoid a hoopla. But compared to Omaha's passers-through and residents, my version of dressing down was their version of dressing up.

I called myself blending in with the crowd when I decided to wear a Juicy Couture sweat suit, a pair of Ugg boots, and Prada sunglasses; but compared to the crowd's ribbed turtlenecks, over-size sweatshirts promoting sports teams, and high-waisted jeans that stopped right at the ankle, I looked like a star.

Riding to O's house in a town called Ralston, I noticed we had passed a Welcome to Iowa sign. I did a double take at the sign and then glanced at my driver, who I immediately began to worry was a crazy serial killer about to kidnap me and keep me captive in Iowa.

"Excuse me, sir," I said, concerned. "We are going to Ralston, Nebraska, aren't we?"

The driver said, "Yes, ma'am."

"Well I could have sworn I just saw a sign that said Welcome to Iowa."

"Yes, this here is Carter Lake. You have to drive through to get to where you're going," he explained. "Many tourists get confused when they see that sign." Then he took it upon himself to give me a brief history lesson. "Back in the eighteen hundreds there were litigations between Iowa and Nebraska about Carter Lake, and finally the U.S. Supreme Court ruled that the city belonged to Iowa. But it's in a weird spot because it surrounds Omaha's airport on the south and the west, making it unavoidable to pass through when you're going to and from."

"Oh," I said as if I cared. *As long as your ass ain't takin' me to some dungeon, I'm cool*, I thought.

After some time, the driver pulled up in front of a small single home on a country-looking road. I looked out the window at the address on the little blue house and indeed it matched the address O had given me. I stepped out the cab and just as the driver was removing my luggage from the trunk, a tall, dark-skinned, curly-haired O came walking through the screen door.

"O!" I squealed, unable to control myself. I ran into his open arms and he squeezed me so tight I thought I'd die.

"What's up?" he greeted me, flashing that same killer smile that he had won me over with years ago.

The driver left my things on the curb and I waited for O to pay him.

O didn't budge, so I paid him myself.

"Enjoy your visit," the driver said as he walked around the car to get behind the wheel.

"Thank you," I told him, then I turned my attention back to my one-time love.

"Sorry I couldn't take care of that for you," he began, referring to the tab. "I lost my damn debit card this morning and I haven't been able to get over to the bank to withdraw any money because my car is in the shop."

All of what he was saying went in one ear and out the other as I couldn't get past the fact that he was alive. I couldn't stop staring at him, and I had a permanent smile on my face from the moment I saw him. The tiny shack of a house and the fact that he hadn't paid for my ride weren't important. I was just so happy to see him. A lot of the feelings I had for that dude resurfaced. And his still being attractive and in good physical shape helped. I felt tingly just looking at him, like a girl in front of her first crush. I was blushing and all.

O took my bags into his house, which was just as small on the inside as it was on the outside. Decorated with floral-patterned upholstered furniture and matching curtains, it looked like the home of somebody's grandmother. However, it was clean. I took a seat on the couch that was against a window, which provided a view of the front porch.

"Look at you," I said, still staring at O.

I must say I was a little caught off guard at O's appearance. The O I knew used to wear colorful minks, matching diamonds, and fresh footwear. I wasn't expecting him to be in a pair of Dickey pants, a flannel shirt, and some scuffed black Tims. But he quickly excused his attire and flashed that smile that made me overlook it anyway.

"I've been working all day," he explained.

"It's cool," I said. "Shit, I still can't believe I'm even here talking to you!"

"I know. It's been a long-ass time," he said.

"Well, are you gonna sit down?" I asked him, wanting to be up under him, dingy and all, it didn't make me a difference.

"I wanna go jump in the shower first, get cleaned up for you."

"Well how about I get in with you?" I suggested. "I would like to freshen up too."

That damn smile again. O led me to his bathroom, where he turned on the shower. He put my bags in the master bedroom against a wall of shutter-covered windows. He then began to undress, throwing his dirty clothes in a laundry basket that was sitting in a corner.

I looked at his body; it was intact. There were no bullet wounds, no scars, nothing indicating the harsh death I had heard he suffered.

"Well, you still look good as ever," O said to me as I too undressed.

"I have to reciprocate the compliment," I told him, stroking his ego.

"And you still know all the right words to say to a nigga too," he added.

I just smirked.

"You had some work done, didn't you?" he asked.

I grabbed my double-Ds and said, "Plenty."

He smiled and said, "They look nice."

"Wait 'til you see the rest," I told him.

"What rest?" he asked.

"I'll save that for the shower," I teased.

O and I stepped into the tub together, where I finally removed my panties and showed O what-all I'd done to myself.

"Oh shit," he said, amazed. "You got a . . ."

I nodded, smiling. "So what do you think?" I asked. "Do you like it?"

O's eyes were bigger than Joan's from *Girlfriends*. He put his hand up to his mouth as if it were a bullhorn and he said, "Hell yeah."

I let out a sigh of relief. It could have gone either way. I mean, it wasn't like O didn't like it when I had my manly parts. It was no telling whether he would be excited or disappointed to find out that I had it cut off.

"Can I touch it?" he asked. His dick started to awaken.

"Please touch it," I told him, desire in my tone.

O reached out and rubbed his fingers over my pussy, particularly stroking my clitoris.

"Can you feel that?" he asked, wondering if I had sensation in that spot like women did.

"Yeah. It's the same nerves that were in my head. It's just disguised as a clit."

"Damn, I missed you," O mumbled as he began touching me all over.

Between the warm water and O's big masculine hands, my whole body was aroused from my nipples to my toes.

"Can I put it in you?" O asked.

"You can do whatever you want," I said.

On that note, O turned me around and bent me over, my hands resting on the back of the tub for support. He gently rubbed his erect penis up and down my vagina, slipping the head in occasionally. I was cherishing every moment of it, yearning for him to put it all the way in me, deep, slow, and passionate.

"Give it to me," I moaned.

"You want it?" he teased.

"Yes. I do. Bad."

"How bad?" he asked, lifting me up and nibbling on my ear.

"Bad as a mothafucker," I admitted.

Just then, O bent me back over and put it in. He started off slow but progressed in speed with each stroke. Before long he was fucking me hard, thrusting his manhood against my newly constructed walls as if he was trying to tear them down.

"O!" I moaned. "O!" I screamed louder, feeling so good I was touching my own self. Haphazardly squeezing my breasts together and rubbing my fingers up and down the slit in my vagina. It was like my body was a wind-up toy, uncontrollable once wound.

O's movements started to slow down as I felt him getting ready to cum.

"I'm tryin' to hold it back," he said right before quivering inside me. "Shit."

"Too late," I teased him as he continued to pump, trying to let off every last drop of semen before he pulled out.

"Whooo!" he shouted after he exited me. "That was some good shit."

"Yes it was," I agreed, standing up straight.

"Give me a hug, man," he said, bringing me into his chest.

The water ran down our naked bodies as we lingered in the shower. I said a silent prayer, thanking God for allowing me to spend this time with O. Then I looked up at my baby and French-kissed the hell out of him. I was serious with it too. I mean I had never kissed a man like I kissed O that night. And he definitely deserved it. He was one of the few men of my collection that I could truly say I loved. And to go from believing for so long that he was not only dead but brutally murdered, to learning that he was actually alive all that time, made me feel a wealth of emotions. I was overwhelmed with so much joy and passion I wanted to be handcuffed to him during my stay. I felt like I didn't want to leave his side—I wanted to touch him constantly and have him touch me back. I didn't want our lovemaking to end. I didn't want our kissing to end. I wanted to share in that incredible bliss for an eternity.

When O and I finally got out of the shower, we were both wrinkled like prunes. The only reason why we did get out was because the hot water had begun to cool and God knows that it was too wintry outside on that February night to be taking a cold shower.

I started to put on my pajamas, but O asked if I was hungry and when I told him yeah, he asked if he could take me out to eat. I was never one to turn down food, plus I was hungry as a hostage, so I put on some True Religion jeans, a True Religion hoodie, and my boots. I threw on my short fox coat to shield me from the winter wind. Meanwhile, O had called a cab to pick us up and take us to a restaurant called the Old Chicago, which supposedly served the best pizza and the best beer. Or so their sign said.

It was at dinner that I finally asked O to explain to me what happened and why the feds had him fake his death.

Drinking from a glass of beer, he began, "I was an undercover DEA agent when I met you."

"WHAT?" I almost choked on my slice of extra cheese. I couldn't believe what I was hearing. O, to me, was a big-time drug dealer who had the whole entire state of Delaware on smash. He was a thug-ass nigga who had money, bitches, and ghetto fame galore.

"Yeah, I was working to take down one of the East Coast's fastest growing drug operations."

"So all that time, you was a fuckin' . . . cop?" I asked, my eyes squinted in disbelief.

O nodded. "Yeah. When I met you, I had just about all the information I needed to build a case. But what happened was I got plugged in with some big-timers in Baltimore."

"Yeah, I remember when you would take trips down there," I reflected.

"And then one of the main guys who was cooperating with us ended up getting killed."

"Who was that?" I asked, curious.

"He was actually a kingpin. He was the only other big-timer besides me in Delaware."

"Ohhh. I know who you talkin' about. He was your only competitor, right?"

"Yeah. And just when we got him to agree to testify, he got killed. That was when we started feeling like my cover was about to be blown. We didn't know how, but we just got all these funny feelings. Things started to change drastically. So, to avoid me being the next one killed or found out about, the feds faked my death and sent me out here in isolation. It was the only thing to do."

"Unbelievable," I said, thinking of all the money O used to make and how well he hid his true self from me and everybody. *If only Tina could be here to hear this shit*, I thought. "So did y'all ever build y'all case?"

"Yeah, they used all the info I had gathered—the wiretaps

and the stuff I had witnessed—to build a pretty strong case. Seventeen people were brought up on indictments and twelve got convicted."

"Daaamn," I said. "I'm glad I wasn't doing nothing illegal around ya ass. I'd probably be in jail right now fightin' niggas off my ass."

O chuckled. "Naw, you was straight. Having you was actually the good part about being an undercover."

"I bet." Still baffled, I asked, "But I don't understand, though. What about your aunt in Delaware and your wife and all your family out there?"

O wrinkled his face and asked, "What aunt and wife?"

"The lady whose name my car was in . . . and ya other two girlfriends, but we won't get into all that."

"Oh, Carolyn?" he asked. "Is that who told you I got killed?"

"Yeah. I figured she was my only hope of finding out something after I heard you had gotten kidnapped," I explained.

"Carolyn wasn't my aunt. She was just a hood chick who was money hungry and would do anything for a couple dollars. She fed that story to the cops about me being her nephew just to avoid jail time for stashing my drugs and shit."

"So that little nice lady was a hustler?"

"Hell yeah. She used to transport for me and everything. Another dude out there who was getting money like that turned me on to her. He told me she was a good source of information. So I used her for all I could."

"Don't tell me she ended up getting indicted too," I said, feeling a great deal of pity for the woman.

"She actually got off lucky. She took a plea bargain; did two years in the feds and got five years' probation."

"Oh my goodness. The shit that goes down in the life."

"Speaking of which, what you been doin' since you thought I was dead? I mean, what the hell took you to Hollywood?"

I sipped my root beer. "Well, where do I start?"

"Whatever happened to ya homey? Ya girlfriend, what was her name?" O cut in.

"Tina," I refreshed his memory.

"Yeah, Tina. Y'all still tight?"

I broke the news to him. "Tina is dead."

"Get the fuck outta here," O said. "Are you serious?"

"Unfortunately," I said.

"Damn, I'm sorry to hear that," he said.

"It's cool," I said. "I'm dealing with it, you know."

"What happened? How did she die?"

"She got shot."

"Naw," O said.

I nodded. "Actually we both did. But as you can see I survived."

O's facial expression grew even more surprised. "You lyin'."

"No, I'm not. I wouldn't lie about something like that."

"Well, what the fuck happened?"

"It's a long story. I really don't wanna talk about it. I try to keep it in the past."

"I respect that," O said, placing his hand over mine and rubbing it. "Damn, life is a bitch, ain't it."

"Sure is," I said. "And she fuck you every chance she get."

"Ain't that the motherfuckin' truth," O said. Then a brief silence ensued while I drank up the last of my soda and O finished his beer.

"So what do you do now?" I asked, switching the subject back to O.

"I'm a truck driver."

"For real? What, after you go undercover once, you stop working as a cop?" I didn't understand.

"No. But in my case, it was best. For my protection anyway."

"So you said you didn't have a wife or any family up in Delaware?"

"Naw. All my family is out in New Jersey, where I'm from."

"Um, that's crazy," I said, referring to O's revelations. "It's funny how you think you know a person. Turns out you really don't know shit."

He made light of his duty. "It's just a job."

"Well, it's a fucked-up one, sorry to say. I mean you put

yourself on the line and get a bunch of convictions, but at the end of the day you gotta desert your family and start your life over from scratch. That sounds unfair to me."

"No lie, that is the hardest part to deal with. I mean, like you said, I put my life on the line for my job and all I got was relocation money and witness protection." O's voice was low, but I could tell he was feelin' that shit.

"Can't you move where you wanna move?" I asked, wondering if O had a choice in the matter of living out in East Jablip.

"They got certain places for you to go. And the more wanted you may be, the farther out they want to send you," he explained.

"But don't you miss your family and being able to live a normal life?"

"Yeah, I do. But to be honest, I been out here so long that I done got used to it. As far as I'm concerned, I *am* living a normal life."

"Well, I guess that's possible."

"Now what about you? You never did answer my question about how you ended up in Hollywood."

"Well, after I had my surgeries I met this photographer in New York who said he liked my look and wanted me to do a test shoot for a real popular fashion magazine. So I did it and ended up being chosen for the spread. From there I started getting more and more print work and I built a portfolio. I used my portfolio to get a modeling contract with an L.A. agency and when they signed me I moved out there. I been hustlin' my way to the top ever since." I delivered the story in a nutshell.

"Damn, that's what's up," O said. "I'm proud of you. I be seeing you all over the TV and shit. I just be laughin', like damn, look at her." Then he looked at me and asked, "So you make a living doing that, huh?"

I looked at him back and answered, "Shit, I make a killin'."

"I ain't mad at you," he said, smirking.

O's eyes were locked on mine. I blushed and he smiled. I found myself in a trancelike state until our waiter came and put the bill on the table.

"Can I get you two anything else?" the tall, thin white guy asked.

"No, thank you," I responded.

"Naw, we're good," O said.

"Okay, well, I'll take that whenever you're ready," he said as he darted away from our table.

O picked up the bill and looked it over. "I can't believe I lost my debit card," he said, reminding me of his moneyless drama.

I reached out and took the bill. "It's on me," I said.

"I feel so bad," he said. "I promise tomorrow I'll go to the bank if I have to catch a cab and I'll pay you back all the money you spent out here."

"It's okay," I repeated.

It didn't matter to me that O was broke. It wasn't like I was looking for him to be my man. It was just good seeing him again and knowing that he was all right. The feelings that I had when I stepped out the cab and laid eyes on him for the first time in years were dying down. I mean he wasn't that ballin'-ass nigga who bought me any- and everything I wanted anymore. Don't get me wrong, I still had love for him, but I couldn't see myself being with him. So at that point his status didn't faze me.

I enjoyed the rest of my visit with O, but when it was time for me to get on the plane and go back to L.A. I felt relieved. I didn't feel so connected to O like I had when I first saw him. Instead, I felt distanced from him, like he was out of my system. I didn't know if it was his bland and not-so-appealing lifestyle that turned me off from on like a light switch or if I just didn't love the new O like I had loved the old O. Maybe it was the combination of the two. All I knew was, saying good-bye to O wasn't difficult at all. I actually felt good about departing. The way I saw it was that I had a mini-vacation that gave me time to vent and get some backed-up cum out of me and now it was time for me to get back to my upbeat life. As I was going through security, O asked if I was going to come back and see him again.

I told him of course, but in my mind I was saying, *Nah*.

The truth was, the time I had taken out to spend with O was just a fling. And no matter how hard I tried to get back the feelings for him that I had before, I couldn't. I was over him. I had come down off my high on him. I was looking at him through sober eyes and realized we were two different people who had gone in two totally different directions. And I felt we were better off staying that way.

March 2007

I couldn't believe my trip to New York to shoot my first feature-length film was around the corner. I had so much to do to prepare. I needed to pack enough clothes for at least thirty days—that meant sixty outfits. I had to give Si-Si the key to my PO box so she could pick up my mail for me. I had to memorize my script and practice it with Si-Si over and over so that I would have it down. I really wanted to put my all into this project—it was the break I needed to make my mark in the business. I had no intentions on treating it like a joke.

Sean was very helpful, shockingly. He helped me study my lines and gave me constructive criticism. We weren't back to normal quite yet, but we were both putting forth the effort, me mostly. Ever since he got back from Vancouver, I'd been kissing his ass. I was trying hard to win him back. I mean there were days I would drive to his house at the crack of dawn with breakfast for him to eat before he left to go to his office and a packed lunch for him to take. I think that's what got him to start talking to me again. Then slowly he started letting down his guard. And we eventually got to the point where we started going out again. As far as the lovey-dovey moments, they were far and few in between. But I didn't sweat it. I couldn't expect him to put the carriage before the horse.

It was a Wednesday afternoon when I got a call from one of the producers on the movie. She wanted to confirm my address so that she could send me a package in the mail with all the vital information I needed for my temporary move to New York: a copy of the script with the shooting schedule, wardrobe selections, and set locations attached; my flight itinerary; my hotel accommodations; meal plan; and covered expense items. Also there would be a checklist for me to be sure I packed everything I would need without leaving anything behind. I was anxious, excited, and nervous all in one. I was ready, but there was one call I had to make first.

"Hello, Ms. Carol?" I asked.

"Heyy, Celess," Ms. Carol sang. "Long time no hear from."

"I know," I said. "I've been a busy lady."

"I know, I know. I see you everywhere. You are really doing your thing."

"Thank you," I said. "How have you been?"

"I've been fine. You know I opened my own practice," she told me.

"Oh my goodness, no, I didn't know that."

"Yeah. I actually just completed the renovations on my office last week. I've been busy too, girl."

"I see. Congratulations."

"Thank you. Thank you," Ms. Carol said, seemingly very happy.

"Well, I was calling to let you know that I'll be moving to New York for about a month or two."

"Really?"

"Yeah, for a movie I'm in."

"You go girl," Ms. Carol cheered.

I chuckled. "Yeah. I landed a lead role in this film called *Gun Play*. So we're scheduled to start shooting next month in Harlem."

"Get out," Ms. Carol gasped. "Well, I am proud of you as always. And hopefully you can make your way down to Philly to see me while you're over this way."

"Yeah, yeah, definitely," I told her. "I know I'll get some breaks between shoots."

"Yeah, maybe you can take the bus down and I'll pick you up from the station. We can have dinner or something. Maybe a drink or two to celebrate our recent accomplishments."

"Sounds good," I said, smiling.

"Well, Celess, I hate to end our conversation, but I have a client about to walk through the door . . ."

"Oh, okay," I said. "Well, it was good talking to you."

"Yes. Likewise. It's always good to hear from you."

"All right, Ms. Carol. I'll talk to you."

"Okay, sweetie. Take care."

I hung up with Ms. Carol feeling good inside. It was such a blessing having her in my life, even if I didn't see and talk to her as much. It was just good to know that if I ever needed anybody she was there. It was like having not only a mother, but a good friend as well.

Just as I was getting up off the couch to go in my kitchen and fix me a sandwich, my cell phone rang. It was Si-Si.

"Hey girlie," I answered the phone playfully.

"Celess, they just took my grandmother to the hospital!" she told me.

"What happened?" I gasped.

"She had a stroke." Si-Si's voice cracked on the word.

"Oh my God. What hospital is she at?"

"We're at Huntington on California Boulevard."

"What's the address so I can put it in navigation?"

"Um, one hundred West California Boulevard, Pasadena."

"All right," I said, scribbling the address on a piece of paper. "I'm on my way."

"Okay."

I rushed and made me a sandwich, eating it as I walked out the door. I was too hungry to wait until I got to the hospital, plus I wasn't a fan of hospital food anyway. I drove to Pasadena in a panic, beeping at everybody in my way, pedestrians and all. It seemed like the whole world moved in slow motion whenever you were in a rush. I got to Huntington and had just parked when my cell phone rang again.

"Hello," I answered, not even looking to see who it was.

"What's up?" O's voice asked.

"What's up, O. Listen, I'm busy right now. Can I call you back a little later?"

"All right."

"'Bye."

I turned my phone on vibrate and went inside the hospital. I saw Si-Si in the Emergency Room's waiting area.

"Thanks for coming up here," Si-Si said, hugging me.

"No problem," I said. "What's going on? Did they tell you anything yet?"

"Well, they said they had to do a CT scan to find out everything," Si-Si said. "My mom just went back there to see what's going on, though."

I huffed and rubbed Si-Si's leg and told her to pray. I sat out there in the waiting room with her and her mom for hours until we were allowed to go back into the ICU room where her grandmother had been situated.

Si-Si's grandmother was lying in the hospital bed with an IV in her arm and an oxygen mask over her face. She looked like she was sleeping. Si-Si's mom broke down instantly upon seeing her mother in such a state. She had to leave the room.

The doctors explained that Si-Si's grandmom had had an

ischemic stroke, that is, one caused by blood clots in her brain. They had given her some drugs to help dissolve the clots but had to monitor her blood pressure closely.

"How long will she be like this?" Si-Si asked.

"It depends on how she responds to the treatment. We just have to take it one day at a time."

Si-Si told her grandmother that she loved her, even though we knew that she probably couldn't hear her. She kissed her on her forehead and rubbed her fingers through her thin, gray hair. Then we left so Si-Si could comfort her mother.

I offered to stay with Si-Si and her mom at their apartment for the night. I figured they could both use some support. I was even going to call a masseuse over to pamper the three of us. Going for my cell, I noticed I had several missed calls and voice mail. I called Sean back first.

"Hey babe," I said.

"You busy?" he asked.

"I just got out of the hospital," I told him.

"Is everything all right?" he demanded, panicked.

"Si-Si's grandmom had a stroke."

"Oh, damn," he said. "Tell Si-Si I'm sorry."

"I will. I'm actually going to spend the night at her house tonight. I know you were supposed to come over and help me with my script, but she really needs me right now."

"Oh yeah, I understand. I'll just get up with you tomorrow."

"All right, babe," I said.

"All right." ,

I hung up with Sean and checked my voice mail.

Message 1 from O: "Hey Celess, it's O. Just calling to holla at you."

Message 2 from O: "It's me again. I know you had said you was busy, and that you would call me back, but I figured you might have forgot, so hit me when you can."

Message 3 from O: "All right. This is my last time bugging you. I found some cheap tickets out here for the end of the month. I was thinking it would be good to see you before you go to New York for your movie. Let me know if you gonna come. I'll pay for your flight."

I got to the last of O's messages and felt stalked. Why the hell did he feel the need to blow my phone up after I told him I would call him back? *I hope he ain't gonna turn into no pain in my ass*, I thought as I booked the masseuse.

I drove to my house to get some pajamas, a change of clothes, and my toothbrush. From there I went straight to Si-Si's house. When I got there, her mom was in bed and Si-Si was going over some papers at the dining room table.

"Do y'all even feel up to massages?" I asked, not wanting to force anything on them.

"I do. She probably don't," Si-Si said, rubbing her puffy, watery eyes.

"You sure?" I asked. "I can call her and cancel before she come out here."

"Girl, I'm positive," Si-Si said. "I'm so stressed right now, a massage would do me just right."

"I bought some wine too. I figured every little bit helps."

I went in Si-Si's kitchen and helped myself to two wine-glasses. I poured us each a glass and went back into the living room. I slid off my flip-flops and sank my toes into the plush berber carpet. I sat back on the couch and sipped the wine.

"You think your mom wants some?" I asked Si-Si.

Si-Si shook her head. "She's probably in there knocked out. She don't like to be around people when she's going through shit. She'd rather be alone."

"I can dig it," I said.

"Thank you, though," Si-Si said.

"It's nothing," I told her.

Ring! Ring!

"Who the hell is it now?" I mumbled, reaching into my pocketbook, retrieving my phone. It was O—again. I wasn't going to answer it just because, but I did want to talk to him and tell him about himself.

"Hello," I answered, purposely sounding frustrated.

"What's up?" O whined. "I've been tryna get up with you all day. I booked you a flight out here in two weeks."

"What?!" Too through, I was about to go off on O, but I didn't want to hurt his feelings. He seemed all excited about what he had done and it would have been wrong for me to curse his ass out about it. So I took a deep breath and tried to keep my composure.

"O, you should have checked with me first," I said. "I have too much to do before I leave for New York to come out there," I explained.

O sucked his teeth. "I'm sure you can get it done before then. I'm only asking for a couple days, that's all."

I rolled my eyes and sat my glass of wine down on the table. "I would, I really would, it's just that I have so much going on. Matter fact, my best friend's grandmom had a stroke today and I was in the hospital with her when you left me all those messages earlier. That's why you didn't hear from me all day. And right now, I'm here with her so I really can't talk."

"Aw, you goin' do me like that?" O asked.

I was caught off guard at O's obsessive behavior. "Do you like what? My best friend needs me right now. How you not gonna respect that?"

O sucked his teeth again. "You just sayin' that shit to get me off the phone. If you don't wanna talk you don't have to. Just be straight-up with me."

"O, on some real shit, you startin' to piss me off. First of all, I don't have to make up lies to get you off the phone. If I don't wanna talk to you I'll just bang on ya ass and let that be that." I smirked.

"Damn, all that?" he asked. "You goin' treat the nigga who made you like that?"

Oh, hell *no*, I thought. I had to step outside in the hall so that I wouldn't disturb Si-Si's mom when I got to cursing O out.

"I know I didn't hear you just refer to yourself as the nigga who made me!" I began. "You ain't been in my life for over five fuckin' years. It's not only a lie that you made me, but it's fucking impossible!"

"What? Who kept you laced when you ain't have shit? Who paid ya bills and kept you in a hot ride? I did all that shit. If it wasn't for all that you wouldn't have ever made it out to L.A.!" O proclaimed.

My mouth dropped, I was so appalled at O's outrageous claims. "Let me clear something up: I was gettin' all that shit done by plenty niggas, not just you! Annnnd, long after you were out the picture I was on top! So please don't flatter yourself with that 'you made me' nonsense!"

"Bitch, is you smokin'? I put you on the motherfuckin' map! It was me who introduced you to being fly. So technically, I did make you!"

I had to set him straight. "Oh, you wanna get technical? Let's get technical. Technically it was the feds' money—not yours—that paid for my lifestyle! And if you should be trippin' on anybody it's their motherfuckin' asses because it's real fucked up that they took better care of me then than they're taking care of you now!"

"You's a nut-ass bitch, you know that? Fuck you. I'll cancel the fuckin' tickets!" O shouted, wounded by my last comment.

"Good!" I shouted. "I ain't plan on coming back to that raggedy-ass house any ol' way." *Click.* I pressed the End button on my phone so hard I could have broken my thumb. I was hot. I could not believe the nerve of O's corny ass to call me and harass me like that. He had lost a million cool points for that nut shit.

"Who the hell was that?" Si-Si asked as soon as I walked back in her apartment. She was pouring herself another glass of wine.

"Some nigga I used to mess with back in Philly—" I began to explain.

Just then Si-Si's doorbell rang. It was the masseuse. And she couldn't be more on time. Si-Si and I both needed a massage at that point.

I let Si-Si go first as I told her about my secret getaway in Nebraska with O. I left out a lot of details for the sake of us not being alone. I didn't like to talk too much around other people because you never knew who knew who. After Si-Si's hour, it was my turn and Si-Si talked to me about her developing relationship with David. Apparently they had been growing more and more attached to each other and she told me that she thought she might be falling in love. I commended her because David was a good catch. He was young, rich, and famous, and he wasn't bad to look at either.

I told her if I was her I would wife that nigga. Having a serious relationship with him would definitely boost her career. Shit, she was already getting lots of free press just by being seen with him. Imagine what would happen if she married him.

Si-Si and I talked until the wee hours of the morning, catching each other up on all the latest gossip. It had been a while since we actually had time like that to spend together. Between us both working so much and spending whatever spare time we had with our boyfriends, we had lacked that "girlfriend time" we used to share. It was good, though, to finally fit it in our schedules. Too bad it had to take Si-Si's grandmom getting sick for it to happen. But that was life. Everything happened for a reason.

April 2007

I checked into the Paramount Hotel on West Forty-sixth Street near Times Square. The production company had a block of twenty-something rooms. I kept trying to figure out how much of a budget they had to shoot the film—I imagined it was somewhere in the millions. Every time I thought about it I got giddy behind the fact that I was the star in a production so big.

I took the elevator up to the fourteenth floor and went to my room. Walking inside, I felt like I could get use to shit like this. I mean, it wasn't anything extraordinary or nothing. But just the fact that I would be able to order room service all day, have my dry cleaning picked up and dropped back off, and enjoy housekeeping each and every morning was what I was talking about. And I would be able to enjoy it all by myself. I didn't have a roommate like some of the crew and cast. Overall, it was peaceful, a retreat away from the hectic and busy outside world.

I unpacked my clothes and put everything in a place as if I were at home. I ordered a turkey club and an iced tea and then got in the shower. I didn't feel like putting on clothes right away so I just lounged around in the complimentary robe. I decided I would eat and take a nap before I went down to visit the set.

I got to the set at close to five o'clock and it was perfect timing because everybody was sitting around eating pizza.

"Hey," Jay greeted me as I approached.

"Hi, Jay," I said. "How y'all doin'?" I spoke to the others.

"Hi," they said.

"So, it's good to see you had a safe flight," Jay said. "You want something to eat?"

"Yeah," I said, looking at the pizza with hunger in my eyes. I was so damn greedy it didn't make sense. And the number one question people asked me in interviews was how I stayed so thin. I couldn't tell 'em. It was a mystery to me.

"Did you check into the hotel okay?" Jay asked, handing me a paper plate with a slice of cheesy, greasy pizza on it.

"Yup," I told him. "Everything was cool."

"That's good. Well, you wanna take a look around the set?" he asked.

"I would love to," I said.

Jay led me to my trailer first, which really blew my mind. I had my own trailer. That was beyond me. I walked inside and it was set up like a small apartment. There was a couch and TV, a kitchenette and a powder room. It was cute.

"You like it?" Jay asked. "This is where you'll spend most of your time between takes," he explained.

"Yeah, it's so cute," I said, looking around.

"So, you ready?" he asked. "We start shooting tomorrow. You got your shooting schedule?"

I nodded my head. "I think I'm ready. I hope so."

"You been practicing?"

"Yeah. Every chance I get."

"Then you'll be all right," he said. "And I'll work with you, ya know what I mean. I'm not one of those directors that throw you out there with the sharks and expect you to hold ya own. I'll guide you through."

"That's good to know," I said. "I mean I got my mind made up to make you proud of me, but at the same time, this is my very first major role, you know, so I'm a little nervous," I confessed.

"That's understandable. I got you," he assured me. "Come on, let me show you the rest."

I followed Jay as he took me to the other trailers where stuff like hair and makeup would be done and wardrobe would be selected. He asked if I had any questions or concerns that I wanted to talk to him about before the big day and I told him no. He assured me one last time that I was in good hands and I thanked him. Talking to him and getting familiar with the set eased my nerves some. I took a cab back to my hotel and planned to get plenty of rest. I had to be back at the set at five the next morning, ready to work. I changed into my pajamas and called Sean.

"This is Sean Harrison and you've reached me at a bad time. Please leave a message and a call-back number and I'll get back to you at my earliest convenience. Thanks."

"Hey babe, it's me Celess. I'm just calling to let you know that I'm here in New York safely and everything is going good so far. I'm about to go to bed because I have to be on set by five in the morning. So, good night. I'll talk to you tomorrow. Love you. 'Bye."

I put my phone on the charger and turned off the light and the TV. I said my prayers and specifically asked God to help me get through my day ahead successfully. Then I was out, sleeping like a baby.

I arrived on the set at a quarter to five. A coffee in hand, I went to my trailer. I wasn't exactly a morning person, so I just knew I would show up to the set cranky and drowsy. But I was excited so I wasn't, until four hours passed and I was still sitting in the same place I had been sitting in since I walked in the door. It was a little after nine and we hadn't shot one scene. I hadn't had any makeup or hair done nor had I been assigned wardrobe. I was pissed, bored, and would much rather have been still asleep in my hotel. Jay came to check on me like ten times and each time he promised me that we were going to get started in fifteen to thirty minutes. I kept telling him it was cool and to take his time, but the real deal was I was ready to say to hell with the damn movie—and it was just the first day!

I called Sean to tell him about the shit and he didn't answer his phone. What kind of games he was playin' I didn't know, but he was playin' them with the right one. *Give me a reason to take my anger out on you, nigga*, I thought. *Just one mothafuckin' reason*. When I couldn't take sitting around anymore, I decided to leave the set and go shopping. Shit, I was losing my patience to the point of being ready to hurt some mothafuckin' body.

I took a cab to SoHo and walked up and down the streets, going in and out of stores buying up all types of shit, shit I didn't even need, just to spend money. Shopping was helping me deal with my anger. I even took time out to get a manicure. Just as I was hailing a cab to return to the set, I got a call from Jay.

"Where are you, baby girl?" he asked.

"Oh, I had ran to the store. I'm on my way back there, though."

"The store? What store?" Jay asked, not so calm anymore.

"I'm like five minutes away," I told him, avoiding the question.

"Celess, we need you for makeup like right now. Why didn't you tell me you were going to the store?"

"I figured y'all was busy. I knew I was coming right back."

"All right." Jay's voice had grown frustrated. "Just hurry and get back. And come straight to the makeup trailer."

He hung up. He was mad, I could tell. But wasn't that the pot calling the kettle black.

I got back to the set and rushed to the makeup trailer, but not before hiding my bags in my own trailer. I didn't want Jay to know that I had actually gone shopping while I was on the clock.

"Tsk, tsk, tsk," a gay makeup artist clucked at me.

"I know. I'm sorry," I told him, being big about the fact that I was in the wrong.

I sat down in the chair; because I was late, I had to get my hair and makeup done simultaneously. Several hours later I was done, looking like I was thirty-five instead of twenty-five. The idea was for me to look like a sexy detective. Well, they had the detective part down, but I was worried about the sexy. *Let's just hope the wardrobe covers that,* I thought, going into the next trailer to get changed. The skirt suit they had picked out for me to wear had to be altered. Waiting for that took an hour and a half. All in all, by the time I was dressed and ready to begin shooting, it was three o'clock in the got damn afternoon. And I was exhausted.

The first scene we shot was quite simple. I had to get out of a car, walk over to a crime scene, ask the cops that were on the scene a few questions, and look into space like I was deep in thought. I figured it would take an hour tops to get done. Who was I kidding? Between shooting from different angles and cutting when someone did something wrong or missed a line, it took fifty-two takes to get the shot. That was fifty-two different times that I had to do and say the exact same thing over and over again, getting my makeup touched up in between.

Then after that we had two more scenes to get done before we could wrap that day and they consisted of more dialogue and more action than the first, so it took two to three times as many takes to get them done. It was two o'clock in the morning when we wrapped for the day. When I got back to my hotel, I didn't even take off my clothes and shower. I fell out in the bed and didn't awaken until my wake-up call came two hours later. I had to get up, get dressed, and leave out to be at the set again at five. While we got started a lot earlier than we did the previous day, we had many more scenes to shoot so we wrapped just as late.

That cycle repeated for the first seven days of shooting. We were on set all day from early in the morning to early the next morning, getting two to three hours of sleep each night. I was eating less and sleeping less, but working more. By the end of the week I was feeling extremely drained. And on top of things, I was no longer at peace having the hotel room to myself. I was getting lonely, missing the hell out of Sean. The seventh night I called him.

"Hey, baby," I said, exhausted, when he picked up.

"What's goin' on?" Sean asked, sounding just as tired.

"Were you sleeping?"

"Getting ready to be," he answered.

"Oh, I'm sorry. You wanna call me tomorrow?"

"Naw, it's cool. I'm surprised you're up. It's later out there than it is here."

"Yeah, we just wrapped. I'm in the cab on the way to the hotel."

"Damn. Y'all had a long day then, huh?" Sean guessed correctly.

"Yup. Five in the morning 'til one in the morning."

"That's how that shit be."

"It's been like this every day so far. That's why I haven't been able to call you since the first day," I explained.

"I know. Believe me, I know."

"I have a greater respect for you and everybody else in this business. It sure ain't all it's cracked up to be. And people be talkin' about entertainers are overpaid, shit, they work hard as hell for that money," I vented.

"Yeah, it's no joke," Sean agreed. "But when your heart is in it, you can't help but grind."

"I guess you're right," I said. Then I blurted out, "I'm so sorry, Sean."

"Sorry about what?" he asked.

"Sorry about anything and everything that I may have done to make you distant from me," I explained, vaguely. I was talking about what I did with Cliff Warner. I had no business cheating on Sean while he was away working his ass off. After going through a week of shooting this movie and seeing all that it takes, I realized that I was dead wrong for what I done. I should have been at home talking to Sean on the phone, encouraging him and maybe even talking dirty to him—anything to bring peace and happiness to his long workday. I'm sure he would have appreciated it, just like I was appreciating being able to talk to him on the phone that night after a long hard day. Just hearing his voice made everything seem better.

"Do you mean it?" Sean asked.

"Yes, I do. And I hope that one day you can find it in your heart to forgive me."

"I hope so too, Celess," Sean said.

On that note, I didn't want to keep Sean up much longer. Besides, I was pulling up to my hotel. So I decided to hang up with him and call it a night.

"Well, I'm about to go in the hotel and go to bed," I told him. "I'll try to call you tomorrow during lunch."

"All right. I'll talk to you then."

"All right. I love you."

"Me too."

I hung up with Sean feeling fucked up. He didn't even say he loved me back. It was cool, though. *I* had fucked up, not him. And all that tough shit I was talking at the beginning of the week about him playing games with the right one went out the window because I had a soft spot for him. I had really grown a lot of feelings for him since arriving in New York. I think part of it was because I was so lonely, and the other part of it was the fact that I was getting to see what it was like being away from the people close to you and working yourself to death for the sake of fulfilling a dream. I just had so much more respect and love for that man now, and it seemed the more feelings I gained for him the more he lost for me. I was getting paid back and it hurt like hell.

Ring! Ring!

I was on set getting my makeup done, so I refused to answer my phone. In fact, I had the gay guy turn it off for me. Whoever it was I would call back later; if it was an emergency it wouldn't have mattered because there wasn't shit I would have been able to do anyhow.

Lunchtime rolled around and I decided to make good on my word that I would call Sean. But before I dialed his number, I noticed I had a million missed calls and a voice message. I skipped checking the message and just called Si-Si back.

"What's up?" I asked her, hoping she wasn't going to tell me that her grandmom had passed away.

"Why the fuck is every magazine out here running stories that you're a fuckin' transsexual?!"

For a minute I almost blacked out. I felt like I was experiencing déjà vu, like it was 2002 and James was asking me shit about me being a man and I was pissing in my pants trying to figure out a way to lie to him.

"WHAT?" I asked, still in character.

"YES!" Si-Si said. "*Us Weekly, People, OK!*—all of 'em! It's front-page news out this bitch!"

"Who the fuck . . ."

"Girl, I'm tellin' you, the streets is buzzin' about this shit too. They makin' you look real bad. If I ain't have sense I would have been up to all their offices shootin' shit up!"

"Si-Si, I can't believe this nut shit! Why would they print some shit like that?"

"I don't know. But I already called a lawyer and he said if it's not true you can sue all they asses. And if I was you, I would!"

"Damn right," I said. "I don't believe it. That's some corny shit."

"I know! And I'm like real pissed off because they all running this blatant lie like it's the truth. Like they can't be sued!"

"Well, when did they start runnin' it?" My head was still stuck on the fact that my business was being put out there for the world to know.

"Today! And it's the talk of the mothafuckin' town! It even got niggas lookin' at me sideways!" Si-Si carried on. "I wish you was here so you could clear this shit up. I really want you to file a lawsuit, straight up. Matter fact, I can have my lawyer friend send you over some paperwork to get the ball rollin'. I'll make him sue the socks off their asses. I bet they'll take those issues off the stands quick. And I would even make them publicly apologize," Si-Si further suggested.

I was flustered. My mind was all over the place. I didn't know how to deal with the news and it wasn't a good time for me to try to figure it out.

"Si-Si, I really can't even talk to you right now. I'm still on set . . ."

"Yeah, I know, and I hate that I had to call you with some bullshit. But, I was like fuck that, it's better she hear it from me than the streets."

"I feel you and I appreciate it. But um, I'll talk to you about it later. I'm gonna sue those bastards for sure, though." I played it off, knowing damn well I couldn't sue because what they printed was the fuckin' truth.

"All right, girl. Well, get back to what you doin'. And don't let this take you out of your zone. Fuck bitches, get that money." Si-Si called herself coaching me.

"I know that's right. I'll talk to you later."

"All right. 'Bye." She clicked off.

"Fuck! Fuck! Fuck!" I mumbled. "Who the fuck leaked that shit?"

Boom! Boom! Somebody was knocking on my trailer door. "Celess, we need you, honey!" a crew member's voice called out.

I tried to clear my mind as I left my trailer. But there was no way in hell I could. Even during shooting, I was thinking about what Si-Si had told me. I was messing up on my lines, unable to concentrate. And the more takes we did, the harder it got for me. I started feeling overwhelmed with anxiety. Jay was beginning to get frustrated with me. He kept yelling "Cut," and each time his voice got louder and there was more anger in his tone. I began to feel dizzy, incoherent, and delirious, thinking about all the things that could happen if it got out that the stories the magazines ran were true. I completely lost focus by like the nineteenth take and the next thing I knew I was on the ground.

I was taken to the emergency room. The doctors told everyone I was dehydrated and exhausted. Although those may have contributed, I knew the real reason for me passing out. And before I could explain it to Jay with hopes that he would empathize with me and cut me some slack, he walked into my hospital room and turned the channel on the TV to *The Insider.*

I looked up at the screen the minute I heard my name. There was a guy clearly in prison clothing on the screen. His face was blacked out and his voice was disguised. But he was talking about me, saying that he dated my friend and that I was the reason why he was serving life in jail. He said he shot me and my friend after finding out we were men. Could it be—Khalil? That mothafucker!

I squinted as I glanced over at Jay to read his reaction. But his eyes were still glued to the TV screen. The next thing I knew I heard a familiar female voice coming from the television. I looked up and saw my got damn mom on the screen. And this bitch was holding up pictures of me when I was a little boy talking about she wished her son would stop living in sin. She had tears in her eyes and everything, putting me on blast in front of the world. I broke down crying watching that shit. It was one thing for Khalil to take his bitch ass on TV and rat me out, but my mom? That was something different. That hit me where it hurt.

I turned to Jay, who had pressed the Mute button on the remote. "Can you give me a minute?" I asked, unable to control my crying.

Jay nodded, put down the remote, and walked out of the room. I immediately picked up the hospital phone and dialed my mom's number, hoping she would pick up. After three rings I started to hang up but I needed her to know some things, so I decided to stay on until her answering machine picked up. Right after the beep I let go.

"Mom, I cannot *believe* you went on national TV and humiliated me like you did. I don't understand you. When are you going to get it? When are you going to realize that I am not your son anymore? I'm not a normal boy, never was, and never will be. And it's not my fault and it's not your fault. It's nobody's fault. It's just the way God made me—you being so much into God should be able to accept that and stop trying to change me. I can't even change me. So why are you trying to force me to? I'm going to be me no matter how hard you try to push me into being someone else. Just get over it, Mom! And leave me the fuck alone!"

Click! I angrily slammed the phone on the hook.

Jay heard the noise and came back in, asking, "What's going on, Celess?"

"Jay, I am so sorry for all this," I cried.

"I just wanna know what's going on," Jay said nonchalantly. "I mean, I'm not even going to lie, this situation of yours is really messing things up."

"I don't know what's going on myself," I mumbled through my sobs. I offered a poor explanation as I drowned in my tears. "I got a call earlier from Si-Si saying that the tabloids was running these lies and now this shit. All I know is that my mom has hated me since I can remember and has always done things to spite me. And whoever that is in the jail suit must be looking for some money and some fame out of lying on me. And I know you're probably contemplating sending me home behind this bullshit, but I really hope you don't."

"Well, I can't say that I'm not shocked to hear this about you and I was furious and upset at first. But as I thought about the big picture, this just means more publicity for the film. So, I couldn't care less about the rumors or whether they're true or not. My problem is with you letting this keep you from being productive on set. My schedule and my budget are both too tight for any unnecessary delays. I don't mean to sound insensitive, but if you don't think you'll be able to focus because of the personal issues in your life, then I need you to let me know now so I can send you home and replace you before we lose any more time."

I wiped my face and brought my crying to a stop. I was shocked that Jay wasn't mad about the rumors but was more upset about me not being able to perform. I was sure I could fix the problem, especially if it meant I could avoid being sent home.

"Jay, I completely understand and I will do whatever it takes to get back to work. If that's all you're asking, consider it done," I said, determined to keep my spot in the film.

"Well then, you'll be on set first thing tomorrow morning ready to go?" Jay challenged.

"I mean," I began, "if it was up to me hell yeah, but the doctor said I won't be discharged until tomorrow."

"Well, I'm not saying to go against the doctor's orders, but you can check yourself out as long as you feel up to it. And as far as that's concerned, there are things you can do to get your energy level back up. I've known plenty of actors who've been exhausted and passed out on sets, and yet they went back to work the very next day if not the same day," Jay explained, removing his navy Yankees baseball cap from his head and rubbing his palm over his waves.

"Well, what did they do?" I asked. "Because I really don't want to hold up the production."

Jay put his hat back on and stood silently for a moment as if he was deep in thought. Then he said, "Naw, you know what, I think it'll be better if you just go 'head back to L.A. and we find somebody to replace you since we're just a week in."

I frowned and asked, "Replace me? For what? If we're just talking about me getting my mind right then it's no need to replace me. I'm sayin', just tell me what I can do. It don't make sense for me to have put in all this hard work for nothing." Tears started to form in my eyes again as I thought about what my mom had done. I felt like if I got sent home I would be letting her win, and that was so not going down. "Jay, listen, whatever I gotta do, I'll do. I want this job more than anything, and if I let it slip through my fingers because of a stunt my mom pulled then I'll be just feeding into her scheme. I can't do that, especially not after I've come so far."

Jay sat down in the chair opposite my bed. "I wanna tell you what to do, but then again I don't wanna be the one to turn you on to some shit. I mean everybody that I've worked with does it, so it's not like a big deal or anything; but at the same time, I don't know where you stand with it. It's kind of hard to explain. But I just think it'll be best for you to sit this one out."

"Jay, whatever it is that I need to do to stay on this project, just let me know and I'll do it, straight up. I'm not goin' home.

I refuse to go home. If I gotta fuckin' jump through flames to get this shit done I will," I told him, again wiping tears from my eyes.

"You sure?" he asked. "I mean, I can see that you want this and I want you to have it, but are you sure you'll do anything?"

With a serious face I replied, "I'm positive."

"Well, check yourself out and come down to the car. I'll have something for you to help you get back on point," he said.

"Okay," I said, already inching my way out of the hospital bed. And with that said, I was introduced to two things that would wind up having a hold on me like no other: cocaine and the unconditional love I would have for it.

May 2007

I'm taxiing now," I told Si-Si. "You gonna meet me at the gate?"

"Yeah. Well, you know, I'll come as close as I can."

"All right. I'll see you in a minute."

"Okay."

I had just landed at LAX. It was bright and sunny outside, reminding me of what I had missed during my thirty days of living in New York. I didn't know why, but it seemed like New York was always cloudy and dreary. It didn't matter, though. I was back home and up from under the dark cloud that had hung over me on the East Coast.

When we were given the green light to unfasten our seat belts and gather our carry-on items, I stood up, ready to get off the plane. I pulled my Louis Vuitton Damier bag from out of the overhead compartment and hastily walked off the plane. Being in first class, I beat the crowd.

I kept thanking God in my head for many things, but namely that I had a safe flight and that I had finished my part in the movie. Damn, I didn't think I would get through it. The rocky start and then the news that completely caught me off guard almost did me in. But I got through it thanks to Jay's suggestion. Well let me rephrase that: because of Jay's suggestion. I didn't know if I was thankful for it. Matter of fact, I'd been questioning my decision to do coke from the very first time. I knew it was a stupid move, but I had the nerve to think that I would be able to use it only to get me through the movie and then leave it alone. But that wasn't the case, because it had been on my mind constantly after I wrapped.

"Hey girlie!" Si-Si squealed when she spotted me.

"Hey Si-Si!" I gave her a hug. A big smile on my face, I said, "Damn, I missed you, girl!"

"Aww," Si-Si said, smiling back. "I missed you too."

"Shit, I'm glad that's over. Shooting a movie is crazy as hell," I confessed.

At first, I told myself that I would make everybody believe that it was all glitz and glamour being the star of a movie, but I was sure that lie would tell all over my face, because based on how strong I felt the opposite, it was bound to show.

"For real?" Si-Si said, walking beside me toward baggage claim.

"Girl, yes. I am so glad to be home."

We walked through L.A.'s busy airport and got to baggage

claim. As we approached the carousel, a guy snapped my picture. Before I could curse him out, other photographers appeared out of thin air, snapping their cameras in my face. Immediately, Si-Si stood in front of me, blocking me from the view of the lenses. But they kept going. Then, as if they weren't already crossing the line, they started bombarding me with questions:

"Celess, is it true that you're a man?"

"What do you have to say about having had a sex change?"

"Were you really born a boy?"

Every single person in the baggage claim area stopped what they were doing and zoomed in on me. I was embarrassed enough to run the hell out of the airport and leave my bags behind and mad enough to start whipping photographers' asses.

"Get the fuck back!" Si-Si yelled at the paparazzi. "Y'all are goin' too got damn far!"

Some photographers obeyed Si-Si's commands and stopped taking photos, but a couple others kept right ahead. I was getting frustrated and the carousel that would deliver my luggage hadn't even started yet, so it was no telling how much longer I would have to stand out there taking abuse from the press.

I looked around trying to find a way out of the madness and decided Si-Si and I should go into the bathroom to have privacy.

I grabbed Si-Si's arm and pulled her close to me. She didn't say anything or ask any questions, she just went along. We were about to enter the restroom when a photographer shouted, "Shouldn't you be goin' in men's?"

That was it, I snapped. I took off one of my three-hundred-dollar flip-flops and threw it full-throttle at his face. It hit his camera lens just as I had wanted it to. He sarcastically said that he was going to sue me and walked away.

Inside the bathroom, I broke down. "This is too much!" I cried. "I didn't sign up for this shit!"

Si-Si felt real bad for me too and started crying with me. And that was something I never seen Si-Si do, not even when her grandmother was in the hospital. I mean her eyes watered, but I didn't see her shed a tear. But that day in the bathroom at the airport, she bawled. I guessed she had a lot bottled inside and that was the time it all poured out.

A few days went by since Si-Si and I had the escapade at the airport. I didn't get sued by that photographer I had thrown my shoe at, but he did make it his business to harass the shit out of me. Everywhere I went, from the supermarket to the gas station, he seemed to be there, taking pictures of me. I tried to ignore him like most celebrities did. I was pretty successful at first, but that only lasted until he brought his ass to my house.

I was in the kitchen minding my own damn business

and that mothafucker somehow someway managed to take pictures of me while I was taking my shots. I didn't have the slightest idea that he was anywhere near my house, otherwise I would have called the cops on his ass and had him arrested. But it wasn't until the tabloids ran a story about me shooting up that I realized he had been there. And I knew it was him because his name was credited for the photo. I couldn't tell you how mad I was. Not only was that nigga invading my privacy, but of all things he caught me injecting myself with my Delestrogen. How was I gonna explain that shit? Every doctor in the world would be able to confirm that transsexuals received Delestrogen shots. My only hope was that the picture hadn't captured the bottle. If not, then I would be able to get away with saying that I was a diabetic or some shit. I was on my way to meet Si-Si to find out.

"Where's it at?" I asked her.

Si-Si handed me the recent issue of *Us Weekly* and we both sat ourselves at a booth in the back of the 101 Coffee Shop on Franklin Avenue. I scanned the image carefully, checking for any telltale signs that I was shooting Delestrogen into my arm. Then I read over the brief article that accompanied the picture. The headline read: *Dope Fiend or Tranny? Which would you want to be when you grow up?*

"Celess," Si-Si interrupted me while I was reading, "I have to go to the hospital to see my grandmom. But here is the information for Blair Berk. He's the lawyer everybody goes to with cases like this."

I took the business card from her, knowing good and got damn well I wasn't going to any lawyer.

"All right. I'll call him."

"And what the hell *were* you doing?" Si-Si didn't forget to ask.

"I wasn't doing shit. This photo is doctored," I came up with. If I told her I was diabetic she probably wouldn't have believed me because that was something I would have shared with her. So I figured I'd go with the next best thing. Plus, doctored photos were a common thing in our business. It wasn't as far-fetched as the diabetes claim.

"What's Sean saying about all this?"

"That nigga is not returning any of my calls. I think he done had about enough of my shit and this ain't helpin'."

"This is gettin' way out of hand. You need to call Berk like right the fuck now," she pressed.

"I am, I am," I told her.

Si-Si stood up from the booth and bent over to hug me and kiss me on my cheek. "I'll call you when I get out of the hospital."

"All right. Tell your mom and grandmom I said hi and I'm praying for them."

"All right."

As soon as Si-Si left I got back into the article, feeling a panic come over me as I read a quote that supposedly came from an ex-lover who didn't want to reveal his name: *I've known Celess for close to six years. When I first met her she was living as a woman, but she still had a penis. Being gay, I didn't mind, so she didn't have to hide it from me. But she hid it from a lot of other guys.*

I racked my brain trying to figure out who could have given that quote, and only two people came to mind, Terry and O. They were the only two guys I had been open with. And since Terry was closer, I confronted him first.

"Terry can we meet somewhere and talk?" I asked, driving down Hollywood Boulevard, cell phone clamped to my ear.

"I'm with Andrea right now. Is it an emergency?" Terry replied.

"Yeah, pretty much. I really need to talk to you."

"Well, you can't come here, that's for sure," he said. "You want me to meet you at your house?"

"No, no," I answered quickly. "The fuckin' paparazzi is probably out there."

"Oh. Well, how about you meet me at Derrek's?"

"Is he home?"

"I don't think so, but I have a key. How long will it take?"

"Just a couple minutes. I just have to talk to you and I don't wanna do it over the phone."

"All right, then. I'll meet you at Derrek's."

"Okay. Thanks."

I was pretty calm, trying to keep it together. My heart was pounding though, and I couldn't seem to slow it down. I turned off Hollywood onto Sunset. It was still early in the day so none of the clubs were open. But I saw the owner of one of Si-Si and my favorite hangout spots taking stuff in and out of his club. I drove past him and honked my horn. He waved and kept doing what he was doing. I instantly got an idea. I made a U-turn and pulled up in front of the club, double-parking. I walked inside the open door.

"What's up, Cal?" I called.

I knew Cal from being at his club so damn much. Our friendship grew as I became more famous. And of course he would bend over backward for me now.

"Hey, Celess." He hugged me. "Long time no see."

"I been in New York," I told him, "shooting a movie."

"Ohhhh. What's up? What brings you in? You know I'd expect you to be home sleeping."

"I was just riding by and I saw you, and I was like I can grab something off him," I told him.

His face balled up as if he didn't know what I was talking about.

I explained myself, somewhat ashamed. "I wanted to buy some stuff off you. Just a little bit. I ran out."

"Ohhhh," he said, catching on. "I didn't even know you did that."

"Just occasionally, that's all," I said, telling him and myself that it wasn't a habit.

"Oh, I know how it goes. I'll hook you up," he said.

Cal went to the back while I went outside to check on my car. When I got back inside, he handed me a small bag of cocaine. He didn't take my money either, he just told me to remember him in the future when I needed some more.

I got in my car and continued to Derrek's house. For some reason I felt better, more composed, the rest of the drive, even without having snorted yet. I guessed it was just the fact that I had the cocaine that made me feel more relaxed and more comfortable. Like I was going to be okay.

I pulled up to Derrek's Brentwood estate; Terry's Mercedes-Benz S550 was in the driveway. I parked behind him and went up to the door. It was open a bit.

"Terry?" I called out.

"Yeah!" Terry called back. "Come on in!"

I walked inside Derrek's house to find Terry sitting on the couch in the living room. His legs were crossed and he was smiling like he was happy to see me.

"How you doin', princess?" he asked in his old-fashioned pimp way.

I was honest. "Not good. I don't know if you keep up with the tabloids, but somebody leaked the fact that I had a sex change and they're running stories like crazy about it."

Terry's smiley face turned into one of shock. "Whaaat?"

I nodded. "They're saying that one of my ex-lovers"—I put two fingers up on each of my hands to make air quotes—"had said that he knew me for six years and when he met me I still had a penis and that I hid it from other guys but not from him because he was gay anyway." I repeated as much of the quote as I could remember.

"That is outlandish," Terry commented, still in shock.

"I needed to talk to you because you're like the only person who I ever dealt with who knew the whole story, you know?" I slow-walked to the accusation.

"Right, right," he agreed. "But if you're thinking that I talked to someone about it, that's not the case."

I didn't say anything. Terry seemed sincere. So the only other person who could have done it was O. And after our falling-out it was likely that he was the culprit. I suddenly got the urge to tend to the cocaine I had in my pocketbook.

"I'm gonna go to the bathroom," I told Terry, indirectly excusing myself.

I was in the bathroom spreading the cocaine out on my mirror when he barged in, causing me to jump up off the toilet seat. My mirror fell to the ground along with the whole bag of cocaine I was ready to snort. Not only was I embarrassed, I was furious.

"What the fuck, Terry?" I shouted. "Don't you know how to fuckin' knock!"

"I'm sorry. I was just checking on you. It's not like I haven't seen all what you have before."

"But still! That's fuckin' rude!" I shouted some more. I was really hot with his ass, I could have punched him in the face.

"I didn't know, Celess," he whined.

I immediately started crying out of nowhere. I felt a head-ache coming on and I was in some emotional pain. I got down on my knees and started scraping up what cocaine I could from the cold marble tiles.

Terry watched me for a minute, then he intervened.

"Celess, honey," he said, lifting me up, "I can get you some more. You don't have to be on your hands and knees trying to scrape it off the floor."

"Just leave me alone," I told Terry, trying to wipe my eyes. "Just leave me the fuck alone!" I screamed at the top of my lungs.

Terry stepped back and put his hand on his forehead. "I said I can get you some fucking more," he said, obviously get-ting frustrated at his inability to help me.

"Well then go get it then!" I screamed again, even louder than before.

Terry left the bathroom. In the meantime, I was crying at myself in the mirror.

When Terry reentered, he closed the door behind him. He was carrying a small black velvet bag. It looked like one of those bags that you put your chips in at a casino. He put the bag on the sink and opened it up. I watched him closely as he took out what looked like a ziplock bag full of coke. It was definitely enough for the two of us to binge, and that's what we did.

I was sitting on the bathroom floor with my back against the wall, looking like I was asleep. Terry was lying between my legs looking up at the ceiling, occasionally dipping his pinky finger in what was left of the pile of cocaine we had spread out on a mirror beside us and taking it to his nose. We were both high as hell and not at all prepared for the wrath we got when Derrek walked in his bathroom and saw us.

"Terry? Celess?" And before we could say a word Derrek blew his top. His face got beet red and his brows furrowed. "What the hell do you got my brother in here doing?!" he yelled, looking at me with angry eyes. "What is this?!" He kicked the mirror of coke across the floor.

Terry jumped up and tried to calm Derrek, but in his position there was no way Derrek was trying to hear him out. So I got up, deciding I would just leave. There was no use in arguing with him when I was in the wrong.

"Where do you think you're going?" he asked me as I attempted to walk past him.

I sniffed and wiped my nose with my hand, dusting off any residue. "I'm just going to leave. I know I'm wrong so I'm not going to argue."

"Wrong?! That's an understatement!" Derrek said. "You're

in *my* house with *my* brother getting him high in *my* bathroom! What the hell is the matter with you? Are you crazy? Where did you get the nerve?" Derrek was pinning the whole situation on me as if I called Terry up and deliberately said let's go get high in your brother's house while he ain't home.

"Derrek, listen," Terry tried to butt in.

At that point I was in the hallway heading for the front door; Derrek was behind me, with Terry in his way trying to keep him back.

"No! I am fucking outraged! And if this crazy bitch thinks she's just going to walk out of here without offering me some sort of explanation, she is fucking insane!"

I turned around and gave him what he wanted. Shit, if an explanation would have gotten me out of there without much more drama then I was giving him one.

"I'm sorry, Derrek," I began. "I just had a fucked-up day today. Somebody leaked to the press that I was a transsexual and I thought it may have been Terry so we came here to talk in private and one thing led to another. We didn't mean for this to happen, I promise you."

"That's it?" Derrek asked, obviously unsatisfied. "You accused my brother of outing you to the press then turned him on to cocaine? Am I supposed to roll over and take that?"

I looked to Terry, who I thought would defend me by at least telling Derrek that he was already a user. And when he looked away from me, I knew I would have to fight that battle on my own.

"Derrek, I'm wrong for my part, yes, but I did not turn Terry on to anything. That was his bag of coke, not mine."

"Yeah, right! My brother never touched drugs a day in his life! I'm around him all the time! He's no fucking drug user and don't you dare try to tell me otherwise!" Derrek insisted.

"All right. You know what? I'm just going to go," I said, feeling like there was nothing more I could say or do to lighten the situation.

"Like hell you are!" Derrek shouted. "Not in my fucking car you won't!" He snatched my car keys from my hand.

That was it. I finally gave Derrek the argument he was fishing for. "What the fuck are you doing?"

"That's my car out there! You wanna go, go! But my car is staying! After you disrespected me and my house like this, you think I'm gonna let you drive around in a ninety-thousand-dollar car that I paid for? You must be smoking more than some fucking cocaine!"

I retorted, "How the fuck do you expect me to get home?"

"That's not my problem, is it? You better walk down to La Brea and hail a got damn cab!"

"Aw, Derrek, give her the keys and let her go," Terry jumped in.

"I'm not giving her shit, Terry!"

I started to tear up as I looked Derrek in his eyes. "Are you serious?" I asked him, my neck rolling. "You gonna take my car from me 'cause your fuckin' brother is a cokehead?"

Derrek shook his head and said, "You are such a disgrace! I should've washed my hands of you when you got Tina killed."

At that remark, I lost it. I lunged at Derrek so fast I couldn't stop myself. I started fucking his old ass up. Then when he ran from me and locked himself in his bathroom, I started fucking up his house, picking up lamps and telephones and throwing them on the floor, knocking down pictures, kicking and punching the walls, everything. Terry tried stopping me but couldn't. The only thing that brought me to my senses was when I heard Derrek on the phone with the police. I got out of there then, knowing that I would have gotten locked up if I had still been there when the police arrived.

I ran down Derrek's driveway and up the winding road. I didn't stop until I reached a major intersection. I looked up and I was on Twenty-sixth Street and San Vicente Boulevard across from the Brentwood Country Mart. I knew I could call a cab from one of the stores over there.

I waited for about fifteen minutes for the cab to pick me up and still hadn't thought of a place for the driver to take me. I couldn't go home because my house keys were on the same ring as the car keys Derrek had snatched from me. I wanted to call Si-Si, but she was probably still at the hospital with her grandmom; plus, I didn't want her to see me like this. She didn't know that I sniffed coke from time to time and this was no way for her to find out. The driver was driving me around in circles for a while before I decided to have him take me to the airport. *Fuck it*, I thought. *I'll just leave this bitch. I need a break from the bullshit anyway.*

June 2007

I had twenty-five hundred dollars in cash on me and close to two hundred grand between both of my bank accounts when I first checked into the Philadelphia Marriott Downtown. Three weeks later, I was down to fifty-two dollars in cash and I didn't know how much I had left in the bank. That depended on two things: my hotel bill, including room service every day, all day; and my regular bills, like my utilities and car insurance, which were all automatically taken from my checking account. The bottom line was I was broke, financially and spiritually. I had spent three weeks in isolation, not seeing or talking to anybody, binging on coke that I got from a random dealer downtown. I was hitting rock bottom and the only person I could think to call was Ms. Carol.

I picked up the hotel phone and through my tearful eyes I tried to make out the cost of a local call. I would have used my cell but it died the day after I checked in and I never got around to buying a new charger.

"Hello, Ms. Carol?" I asked as if I didn't know her voice.

"Celess?" Ms. Carol asked back. She sounded like she had been wakened out of a deep sleep.

"Yeah, it's me," I said, my voice cracking.

"Is everything all right? It's three in the morning," Ms. Carol informed me.

"Is it that late?" I was really unaware. I mean the alarm clock was sitting right there on the table beside my bed, but I didn't look at it before I called Ms. Carol. I was just feeling terrible and needed somebody to talk to.

"Yes," Ms. Carol confirmed. Then she said, "Oh, but it's what, only midnight in L.A., right?"

"Um, yeah, I think so," I said.

"Celess, are you all right?" Ms. Carol asked with a boost of concern in her tone.

"No. I'm not." I started to cry.

"What's the matter?"

"I think I have a problem," I admitted.

"What kind of a problem, Celess?"

I didn't want to say the words, but they were running around in my head so I just spit them out. "A drug problem," I told her.

"What kind of drugs? Pills?" she guessed.

"No. Cocaine."

"Oh Jesus," Ms. Carol blurted. "Okay. Do you know of a detox center near your house?"

"I'm not home," I told her.

"Then where are you?"

"I'm in Philly."

Ms. Carol's voice rose like ten notches. "You're here?"

"Yeah. I'm at the Marriott hotel downtown."

"Well, okay. Let me make a phone call. Stay put, okay, and I'll call you right back."

"All right," I said. "But my cell phone is dead."

"I'll call your hotel room. You checked in under your name, right?"

"Yeah."

"Okay. I'll call you right back."

"All right."

From the time Ms. Carol hung up to the time that she called me back, I paced my room, biting my nails. I was so antsy and so agitated it was hard for me to be still. Ms. Carol called me back about twenty minutes later with an address to a detox center close to the hotel. She arranged for a cab to pick me up from the hotel and take me there, and told me I could come stay with her after I got out. I thanked Ms. Carol and hung up with her.

Before the cab came I finished up the last of the eight ball I had copped earlier. I swore to myself that it would be my last hit. I gathered my razor, my straw, and the rest of my paraphernalia and threw everything in the trash can. When I washed my face to try to look presentable, my nose started bleeding. I sat on the toilet and held my head back to try to stop it. I ended up taking a wet washcloth with me out of the hotel room, holding it to my nose to catch the blood.

I went down to the lobby and checked out. My bill was sky-high but I was in no position to review it closely and question anybody. So I took it on the chin. I didn't leave without noticing the strange looks I was given by the staff, especially the woman who checked me out. I didn't know if she was looking at me weird because I was famous or because I was holding one of their rags over my bloody nose. Either way, the bitch was looking at me wrong.

I got into the cab and he drove me a short distance, letting me out on Walnut Street, not too far from the hood I used to hang out at, where I learned all about dressing up and trickin'. I was hesitant about going inside the center, but something had to give. I had become a drug addict, going down quicker than I could control, and at the bottom was not where I wanted to be. So it was detox or else.

Withdrawal was hard but bearable, and after seventy-two hours I was free to go. From there I went to the Guadenzia treatment center on Broad Street. I checked myself out after two weeks. It was recommended that I stay longer, but I felt good being sober, so I was fine with going to Ms. Carol's.

First, though, I went shopping. I needed a new wardrobe.

Mind you, the only clothes I had when I flew out to Philly were the ones on my back. I did buy others when I first got in town, but not much. I went to the King of Prussia Mall and hit up Neiman's for shoes, Bloomingdale's for shirts and dresses, and Nordstrom's for jeans. I picked up a few side items, like a hot-ass dress with shoes to match from Versace and a cute shirt and skirt from Donna Karan. Then I hit up Louis for some luggage so that I would be able to get all my stuff back home. I grabbed something to eat from the food court, feeling better than ever—refreshed. When I got to Ms. Carol's she hugged me so tight I was losing oxygen. She looked me over, and with glassy eyes and a half happy, half sad face, she gripped me up again.

She helped me get my shopping bags out of the car I had rented. Then she showed me to the room that I would be sleeping in. I put my stuff up and joined her at her kitchen table to talk.

Ms. Carol wanted to know everything from how I got started with cocaine to how I ended up in Philly with no clothes. I told her too. There was no sense in lying. The story was bound to be breaking news one day. She might as well have heard the truth from me first.

After reliving the crazy, quick addiction I had, Ms. Carol asked if I would go out with her that Friday evening.

"Where are you going?" I asked, eating a forkful of grilled salmon Caesar salad.

"A book release party downtown."

I frowned. "A book release party? Ms. Carol, you must be getting old," I teased.

"Uh-uh," she disagreed. "Going to a book release party don't make you old. Plus, the girl who is having it is a baby, about your age. She's a local author and she's known for having big parties. This'll be her third one." Ms. Carol ran it down while handing me a flyer for the party.

I looked it over. This real pretty girl, in a minidress with diamonds galore, was posted up on a Maybach coupe. *Oh okay,* I thought. *Books ain't what they used to be.* I figured I could chill with that type of crowd. Ms. Carol had done so much for me, the least I could do was go out and have a good time with her.

It was a good thing I had gone shopping because now I had a few dresses to choose from to wear to the party. The flyer said the dress code was sexy. They didn't know that that was my forte. I put on my new Versace dress. It was cream halter style with sequins. The front plunged almost to my waist, revealing every bit of cleavage I had to offer. The rest of the dress fell simply to the middle of my thigh, fitting my body like a glove. I put on the pair of nine-hundred-dollar cream-and-gold Versace stilettos with a plain strap across the toe. The wow factor was created by the gold V that sat front and center on the ankle strap. I wore my hair back and put on a small gold headband. My makeup consisted of smoky eyes, fake lashes, a little blush, and a nude lip. I wore all gold and diamond jewelry, which I had run out and bought from a guy named Alex, a well-known jeweler in the city, after Ms. Carol invited me to the party. Turned out he was sponsoring the event, so he gave me a good price on all my shit.

Ms. Carol and I drove to the Independence Visitor Center on Sixth and Market streets, her fulfilling the grown and me fulfilling the sexy. We parked in the lot and after waiting too long for the elevator, we took the stairs up to the place. We walked to the front entrance and handed over our tickets. The line was long as hell, but for some reason I was escorted to the front along with Ms. Carol. When I got up there I realized why. The got damn nigga at the door taking tickets was the dealer that was serving me when I first got back to Philly.

Immediately my heart started to pound and I felt myself beginning to sweat. Despite that, I cracked a smile.

"Hey Nico," I said, half hugging him.

Nico hugged me back. "What's up, ma?" he greeted me with his Puerto Rican accent. "Y'all two good," he said. "Here, let me give y'all VIP bands." He wrapped a yellow band around each of our wrists. Ms. Carol was delighted, feeling special that we were getting treated like stars, overlooking Nico sliding a nickel bag of coke into the palm of my hand.

I wanted to give it back to him, but I didn't want to draw attention to myself, so I just tossed it in my pocketbook before anyone could see it.

"Good seeing you again," Nico said to me.

I nodded and smiled, but felt like crying. Nico knew what he was doing. He knew that when he didn't hear from me in so long that I was obviously trying to get clean. He never gave me any for free before so why was he giving it to me now? To get me back hooked so I could continue to lace his pockets. He wasn't shit. And I saw right through his trick. Ms. Carol, still giddy, thanked Nico and told him how sweet he was. He told her it wasn't a problem and directed us to the stairs that led to the main event.

Walking up to the party, I was no longer confident. I was paranoid, thinking about where and when I could sneak off and get rid of the blow in my bag. I didn't want to keep it there because during the course of the night, Ms. Carol might have needed something out my bag and found it. Then she would have thought I was playing her all along and that I was still using. I didn't want her to think that, especially since it wasn't the case. Plus, I didn't want the shit near me, let alone in my possession. The thought of it being in my reach was driving me crazy.

"You wanna sit down?" Ms. Carol yelled over the loud music.

"Yeah," I said.

She led me over to a table that had two available seats. It gave me time to notice the orange and white decorations—which were elaborate, by the way. It looked like I was in an

L.A. or a Miami nightclub. I was impressed. I never expected a book release party to be like that. There was a line of people waiting in front of a white tent to get their books signed by the author, who was sitting on a white couch inside the tent. It was hot how it was set up too. And the author chick looked cute. She had on this metallic red minidress, similar to the silver one she had on in the flyer. I think it was leather. She had on a pair of red patent leather Dolce & Gabbana shoes to match. Diamonds were her accessories. She looked hot, I couldn't lie.

"Celess, I'm going to go get my book signed," Ms. Carol said, holding up a copy of a book entitled *Mommy's Angel*. "You wanna go up there and meet the author?"

I started to say yeah, but it clicked that this would be the perfect opportunity to go and discard the coke.

"No, that's all right. I'll wait until the line dies down."

"You sure?" Ms. Carol asked.

"Uh-huh," I said. "Plus, I gotta go to the bathroom anyway."

"You all right?" Ms. Carol asked, giving me a look like she wanted to ask me if I was going to the bathroom to treat my nose.

I nodded and lowered my eyebrows, trying to convey that I was serious when I told her that I was absolutely fine in that regard.

She took my word for it and went up and took her place in

the line. I walked out of the room and onto the balcony. There were a lot of people out there but none at the edge. I figured I could throw the coke over and no one would ever know who did it or what it was. I mean, we were up pretty high. But if it fell on somebody's head or some shit, that would be drawing. Flushing it would be easiest. I went back into the building and asked a guy standing by one of the bars where the restrooms were. He told me downstairs by the entrance.

I walked down there and went in the ladies' room, passing so many people on my way. I still couldn't believe that a book party was doin' it like that. I was glad I wore what I did. I would have been salty if I'd underestimated and just threw on something.

The bathroom was crowded too. Girls were primping themselves in the mirrors and others were actually using the bathroom. I waited a while for a stall to become available and when one did, I rushed inside. I opened my pocketbook and dug around until I got my hand on the small baggie. I looked at it and was overcome with an incredible sensation. I told myself to just throw the shit in the toilet and flush it, but then something inside me said snort it so I could loosen up and have fun. After battling with myself, I stuffed it back in my pocketbook, intending to give it back to Nico. I figured that would show not only myself how strong I was, but Nico too, and then he would have no excuse to offer me the shit again.

I left the bathroom and looked for Nico at the ticket table.

He wasn't there. I asked around for him and somebody pointed me in the direction of the parking garage. They said he had to get something out his car.

I started to wait for him to come back, but I was getting too anxious. My mind was racing with thoughts and ideas of what I should do with the drugs. I tried to ignore the cravings, kept telling myself to just go back to the bathroom and flush it. But my body just walked out toward the staircase that led to the parking garage. Once inside the staircase, I was finally alone. There was no loud music, no crowds of people. I decided it was the perfect place to get rid of the coke. I took it out my pocketbook and quickly opened the baggie. I stuck my pinky nail inside it and put the powder up my nostril. I sniffed with all my might. I repeated those steps in quick, short intervals and started to feel myself gaining control.

After like my twentieth dip, I heard the door to the staircase open. Two guys damn near fell through it, hugging each other at the waist and kissing each other on the lips, both appearing highly intoxicated. Startled, I dropped the baggie. At the sight of me, the guys quickly disengaged and one of them exclaimed, "Celess?"

I looked at him closely trying to make out who he was. "Michael?" I asked, completely surprised.

I could not believe that of all people it was my ex being touchy-feely with another nigga. After he'd told me to kill myself for being a guy!

"What the hell?" He looked down at the cocaine and then back up at me.

I was stunned, stiff, and speechless to see the man I had both love and hate for. I didn't say anything.

"Who're you?" the guy Michael was with asked.

Michael put his hands over his flushed, drunken face. He didn't respond to the guy. The guy then turned to Michael and asked again, "Who's she?"

"My old girlfriend," Michael responded with what appeared to be grief in his eyes.

"Well," the guy huffed, "are you gonna stand here and stare at her for the rest of the night or are you leaving with me like you started to?"

Michael took a deep breath and started to say something but that's when I butted in.

"It's not like that," I told the guy. "Y'all can go ahead."

"Excuse me, sweetie," the guy said. "But I believe I was asking Mike the questions." He had so much attitude and sass it was crazy, especially since he was dressed like a gangbanger. You never would have known he was a queen. I would have had it out with him and treated him like the bitch he was acting like but I was high and still in shock from seeing Michael face-to-face, so I kept my cool.

I headed up the stairs to go back into the party. As I passed Michael and his friend, I mumbled, "I didn't come here for this."

Michael grabbed my arm before I could open the door and said, "Wait. I need to talk to you."

"What?!" Michael's friend flipped out. "This is how you gonna do me, Mike? I'm out then, straight the fuck up. No nigga puts nobody in front of me, especially not no bitch!" The guy gave me the evil eye as he brushed past me and proceeded down the flight of stairs. "Your loss!" he shouted from halfway across the parking garage.

"Oh my God," Michael said. "Oh my God. Why me? Celess, what you saw wasn't what you saw," he tried to explain.

"What did I see?" I asked him, trying to make sure I wasn't just that damn high.

Michael covered his face with his hands again and leaned back against the concrete wall. "Just a friend of mine I haven't seen in a while."

"A friend? Oh okay," I said, not convinced. "Well, excuse me, I'm going back into the party."

"No. Wait," Michael said. "You don't believe me or something?"

"Does it matter?" I shot back, unsure of why Michael cared what I believed or what I didn't. "You hate my guts, remember? You want me to kill myself. Why does it matter what I think or what I saw? Why are you even bothering to have this conversation with me? Why don't you go chase down your piece of ass and let me go about my business?" I asked. I had the nerve to be upset. I figured if Michael was gay then all he had to do was tell me and we could have maintained our relationship. Shit, had that been the case, things would have been a lot different. At least I wouldn't have gone through half the shit I had since his phone call telling me to kill myself.

Michael removed his hands from over his face. "Why are you questioning me? You're the one out here snorting fucking coke!"

"What?" I frowned and chuckled at the same time. "What are you talkin' about?"

"You know what I'm talkin' about! That white shit on ya nose! You a damn drug addict now?"

"You a damn faggot now?" I shot back.

Michael shot a look at me that could have cut me in half. "Bitch, don't you ever make ya lips up to call me a faggot when you're the one who went around suckin' other niggas' dicks for a dollar."

"That's right and I was damn good at it too! Ain't that right, *Mike*?" I snapped.

Pop! Michael smacked me across my face, blowing my high.

"All right, that's the fuck it!" I shouted, feeling blood on my bottom lip. "I'm gonna go get a nigga to whip ya ass! Who the fuck do you think you are putting your hands on me like that?!"

Just as I was starting to open the door and sic Nico on Michael a few girls appeared out of nowhere. They were walking toward the staircase from the garage, apparently just getting to the party. Michael obviously didn't want them to know that we were arguing and that he had busted my lip because he pulled me into his arms, burying my face in his chest. He rested his head on top of mine as the girls excused themselves and passed by us. When they disappeared I lifted my head to get Michael up off me. Tears pouring down my face I asked, "Why did you do that, Michael?"

"I'm sorry," he blurted out, pulling me into him again.

His voice cracked as he asked me, "Why the fuck were you puttin' that shit up ya nose, Celess?"

"Because of you!" I yelled, feeling myself getting angry and agitated as a desire to get high began to burn inside me.

"Because of me?" Michael repeated, surprisingly remaining calm. Backing me away from his chest so that he could look me in my eyes, he continued, "How because of me? I didn't make you do drugs!"

"No, but you sure as hell contributed," I said keeping my head down and eyes to the floor.

"How did I contribute, Celess?" Michael probed, still with a crack in his voice.

I looked up at Michael and started to cry recalling the last words I'd heard him say to me. "All the fuckin' hateful comments you made to me when I was at my weakest point.

Do you know what kind of psychological shit you put me through?" I finally got the chance to confront Michael about how he had hurt me.

"Oh, so you being a drug addict is my fault? Well then I guess we're even because me being a *faggot* is your got damn fault!" Michael appeared to be fighting back tears. "*You* fucked up *my* life, Celess, and you're yelling and screaming at me like I did something wrong! Fuck you! Who the fuck do you think you are?" Michael shoved past me, going toward the stairs. "I made you do drugs," he mumbled.

I grabbed his arm and stopped him in his tracks.

"Michael, stop," I told him. "I am so sorry," I cried, accepting that *I* had turned Michael gay.

"You don't know how to be sorry," Michael said. "You have no fuckin' idea."

"I do! That's why I'm here in this fuckin' stairwell, snorting this fuckin' powder like my life depends on it knowing good and got damn well it's going to take control of me all over again! Don't you see this *is* me being sorry? Me being a sorry ass!" I cried.

Noise came from the other side of the door we were standing a few feet from. Apparently people were about to come through. Michael wiped his face. Then he grabbed my hand and without saying anything more led me down the stairs, into the parking lot, and over to a champagne-colored Mercedes CLS. He opened up the passenger door and put me inside.

He got in the car and started up the engine, wiped his face once more, and drove off.

I didn't ask him where he was taking me. I didn't even tell him that I had come with Ms. Carol and that I should tell her I was leaving before I just left. All I did was space out, forcing my mind to take me back in time to the days with Michael when we were the happiest fuckin' lovebirds you could meet. I reminisced about the time he surprised me and opened me the hair salon in Northern Liberties, the day at the Harbor, all the nights we spent together throughout the cold winter, our first time making love, him being with me at Tina's wedding, everything. It made me go into a crying spell. I felt sorry for myself for fucking all that up. Once again I felt like a failure. Once again I was reminded of the stupid and hurtful shit I did to people. Once again I pitied myself, and contemplated how I was going to end my life.

July 2007

*M*ichael and I spent a whole day at his house with-out saying anything to each other besides the basics: hey, you want something to eat? Pass me the remote. It was as if we were a bickering married couple who hadn't yet made up from a fight.

I called Ms. Carol, who was worried out the ass, to tell her that I was with Michael and I would be staying with him for a couple days. She flipped out at first: one, because she was mad that I had left her at the party without any notification, and two, because I was with Michael. She knew that he was the one who'd driven me over the edge, causing me to overdose on my painkillers, and she didn't know what he was liable to do with me. I explained to her that I was fine and that Michael and I were reconciling. She didn't let me get off the phone with her without first making me give her Michael's address, telephone number, even the license plate number off his car.

It was July 1, a Sunday, and Michael had just come back from the supermarket. The both of us were completely sobered up and I figured it was the perfect time to discuss everything. I approached Michael while he was in the kitchen putting the groceries away.

"You need help?" I asked, standing in the doorway dressed in one of his T-shirts.

"I'm cool," he said, obviously unwilling to knock the chip off his shoulder.

"Michael, it's going on two days and we haven't talked about what happened. There's no way we can keep this up."

"Keep what up?" he asked, stubborn as a mule.

"Keep up this," I said, "this no communicating. We need to sit down and talk. Hash out our differences. Clear the air."

Michael paused in the middle of putting a carton of orange juice in the refrigerator. "Okay, you wanna talk, then talk," he said.

I ignored his attitude and decided to be the bigger person. Besides, it was my fault we were in this predicament, not his. I was the one who deceived him in the first place. I was the one who got us to this point.

"Well, first of all, I want to again apologize. Second, I want to let you know that what happened the other night is in the past and forgotten. Whatever you are doing with your life is none of my business and I hope you feel the same about me as far as what *you* saw. I just really want us both to get past it and to move on. I know neither of us can change any of it, but the least we can do is squash it. I'm talking about all of it—the fight that broke us up to the phone call I got from you after the shooting to everything we said to each other Friday night in the stairwell." I ran it down.

Michael closed the refrigerator and leaned his back against it. He rubbed his bald head, thinking about what I had proposed. He looked at me, then rubbed his goatee.

"All right," he finally said. "We can do that. But for the record, I never did anything with that guy." He shook his head. "I did think about it and I was drunk as hell and dealing with a lot of emotions, but it never got further than what you saw."

I put my hands up as if to stop him from explaining himself. "It really doesn't matter," I told him. "I'm just glad we can get past it all because I really don't want you as an enemy. Believe it or not, I had a lot of love for you and still do to this day."

"I have a lot of love for you too, Celess, and you know that. That's why it hurts so bad that we're not together. I mean it was like I had finally found the right one for me and I did my best to make it work and make it last and make you so happy. And then out of nowhere you were telling me you were leaving me and moving to L.A. with Tina and that I couldn't come with you because you were really a man. That shit took me to left field. I didn't know how to deal with it—I still don't know how to deal with it. It's a struggle, you know. And that shit you saw the other night is what's worst about this whole situation. I was never gay. I never found myself attracted to guys. Just hearing myself say it is making me pissed off." Michael paused and shook his head. "I don't even wanna talk about this shit no more."

I walked over to him and hugged him. I felt so damn bad for him. I didn't know what it was like to be turned one way after being another my whole life but I could imagine it was difficult as hell. I couldn't say that I knew how Michael felt but I wanted to offer some words of comfort.

"I know it's hard, believe me," I told him. "But maybe it's best that you do talk about it. Maybe you need to get it all off your chest."

Michael hugged me back and continued to tell me how I had affected him.

"It was like after you I couldn't find satisfaction from a woman anymore. And it wasn't like I didn't try, because I've been with many. But for some reason I couldn't stop thinking about you. And none of the other women I've been with have measured up to you. So the more I thought about it the more I started thinking that the reason I couldn't find a woman who made me feel the way you did was because you weren't really a woman. And it bugged me out because I started telling myself that I must be gay for constantly thinking about a man. I wondered if I would find what I was looking for in a man since I had found everything I wanted in you. I was confused and hurt at the same time. That was why I called you saying all that stuff like I did. I felt like you destroyed my whole life in an instant, and I wanted you to know how I felt about that shit. That was some fucked-up shit to do to a man, especially an honest one like me," Michael vented.

I heard Michael out and didn't once interrupt him. I wanted him to let out all his feelings because I believed that was what he needed to get past what I did to him. I wanted so bad to fix him—to make the pain and hurt go away and turn him back to the person he was before I corrupted him. I even had the audacity to think that if I gave him some he would go back to liking pussy. It was a stretch but I tried it anyway.

I stood on my tippy toes to reach Michael's lips with mine. I kissed him softly, basically pecking at his lips. He didn't kiss me back at first and seemed standoffish. But I just grew more aggressive, plunging my tongue into his mouth. It wasn't long before Michael started kissing me back. Closing my eyes, I savored every moment of the long and passionate kiss I was getting to share with a man I had so dearly loved. I began to rub my hands up and down his chest and he returned the gesture. Grinding against each other, we slid down the refrigerator and ended up on Michael's kitchen floor—him on his butt with his back against the refrigerator and me straddling him. We stopped kissing for a moment and gazed into each other's eyes. There was a passion present that couldn't be denied no matter what hate or ill feelings we had toward each other.

"I think I still love you," Michael said, a tear slipping out the corner of his eye.

"I know I still love you," I told him back, holding his head in my hands and kissing him repeatedly on his forehead.

"What am I going to do with you?" Michael asked.

"Make love to me," I suggested.

"How?" he asked? "You're a . . ."

"A woman now," I finished his sentence, guiding one of his hands under the oversize T-shirt, between my legs.

Michael closed his eyes as if he was in fear as he reluctantly rubbed his hand up and down my vagina.

"See," I said. "I'm a woman."

Michael opened his eyes in amazement. He continued rubbing me as he mumbled, "You are a woman. And you've always been a woman. I'm not gay. I love your pussy. I always have. I just got confused, that's all. But now I'm back. I'm all right. I know what I've been looking for all that time and it wasn't a man. It was you. It was you, Celess."

"I know, baby," I mumbled back, getting aroused. "I know."

I started gyrating, practically giving Michael a lap dance. In return he slid his hands up my shirt and caressed and sucked my breasts. I felt him getting hard beneath me and I was over-come by a sensation for him to be inside me. I abruptly stood up, making Michael grab my calves as if he was trying to pull me back down. Keeping my balance, I pulled the shirt up over my head. Then I slowly and seductively pulled my panties down my legs. And even though Michael had already touched it and rubbed it, I could tell that he was surprised to see that I really had a vagina.

Pulling my naked body back down on his lap, Michael whispered in my ear, "Tell me I was having a nightmare. Tell me that you've always been the woman I'm seeing today."

"Shhh," I whispered back. "Everything starts from now. Nothing else matters."

Michael unbuckled his belt, then unbuttoned his jeans. He pulled his erect dick from the slit in his boxer briefs. Jerking it a few times, he guided it toward my entrance. Slowly he entered me, making me feel every inch of his solid penis. I held on tight as if I was on a ride as Michael lifted his bottom half up and down on the kitchen floor. I was feeling so good, I cried. Emotionally and sexually I was redeemed.

Michael came inside me and mumbled something about him wishing I could have his baby. I was enamored of the thought of such a wonderful thing and silently wished I could too. Then after moments of just resting in each other's arms, we got up off the floor and headed upstairs to Michael's master bath. We took a shower together and made love for the second time, that time lasting twice as long as the first. We both were exhausted at that point and after drying off and throwing on clean T-shirts and boxers, we both lay down in Michael's bed. We slept peacefully for hours.

When we awoke, it was four in the afternoon. Michael got up to start dinner. I wanted to stay and eat with him but I figured I needed to leave while we were still on good terms. The longer I stayed with him the more likely it was for either of us to start thinking about old shit and possibly start up another argument. I felt it would be better for us to part ways as friends rather than enemies. I put my Versace dress and shoes back on and Michael drove me to Ms. Carol's. We exchanged another passionate kiss before I got out of his car.

"Thank you, Celess," he said as I opened the passenger door.

"For what?" I asked.

"For helping me realize that I could get my life back."

I smiled and thanked him for doing the same for me. I told him I wanted us to keep in touch and he agreed. I got out of the car, closed the door, and waved good-bye, feeling a great deal of relief and a sense of happiness that I'd come to believe I was exempt from.

After answering a series of questions from Ms. Carol and settling down, I checked my bank accounts. My funds were in sad shape. It was time for me to face reality and get my life back in order. I immediately went to the nearest RadioShack and bought a charger for my phone. I plugged my cell up as soon as I got back to the house and when the charge was full I called Si-Si.

"Bitch, where you been?!" she screamed in my ear.

"I'm sorry," I said. "I had to get the fuck away."

"Get the fuck away? Where are you at?"

"Philly."

"Philly? You picked up and took ya ass to Philly without giving me a phone call, a letter in the mail, not even a text, nothing? Just pick up and leave Si-Si all by herself and have her going crazy looking for you!"

"I know. I am so sorry. I am horrible friend."

"Bitch, I done reported you as a missing person and everything!"

"Oh my God, Si-Si, you did for real?"

"Hell yeah. I ain't know what happened to ya ass. Nobody had seen or heard from you! Ya car wasn't in ya parking space at ya house. You wasn't picking up ya mail from the post office! And I was like something gotta be wrong, this bitch ain't picking up her mail. Not the way she be looking for those checks."

Si-Si knew me well because that was one thing my ass wouldn't neglect come hell or high water. I was gettin' my mail. "Aww, Si-Si, I swear to you I am sorry. I just had to leave. I had a falling-out with Derrek and I just had to go. I was on the brink of losing my got damn mind," I explained.

"Well, what the hell happened? The last I talked to you, you was supposed to call the lawyer up about the rumors and straighten that shit out. Next thing I know, I'm calling you and gettin' ya voice mail. I'm leaving you messages and not hearing back from you. A whole month has gone by, and I'm like what the fuck?"

I shook my head as I listened to Si-Si. "Yeah, I shouldn't have done you like that. My cell had died, but I could have called you from a landline," I admitted. "I just been going through some shit."

"Like what?" Si-Si asked.

"Si-Si, I don't even know where to begin," I told her.

"Well, you can start by telling me more about this nigga O you snapped on that night my grandmom got taken to the hospital. When I didn't hear from you I started picking ya mail up for you and I kept seeing letters from him so I decided to open them, wondering if he had anything to do with you being gone. He wrote you about a thousand crazy letters about him being the one who leaked your secret to the tabloids and saying shit like the same way he made you is how he can break you. What the fuck is that about, Celess?"

"So it was O," I thought aloud.

"Celess, is there something you wanna tell me?" Si-Si asked bluntly.

I didn't know how to respond to her at first. I mean the girl was no dummy and the facts that I hadn't jumped on getting a lawyer to dissolve the rumors, then disappearing, and now the letters from O were all pieces of a puzzle I was sure she was starting to put together. On the other hand, though, I still didn't know her enough to be able to trust her with my secret.

I mean that was vital information, and it was already in the wrong hands and shit could get even more ugly.

"Seriously, Celess," Si-Si pressed. "What is going on with you? 'Cause the rumors are spreading like wildfire out here, and with you leaving like that everybody's taking them to be true. They even pointin' fingers at me like I'm a man or some shit. I even got denied a gig for this shit."

"No the fuck you didn't," I said.

"I lie to you not. That's why I was panicking out here. I was like where the fuck is she? She need to clear this shit up before we both be out of commission."

The rumors were starting to affect Si-Si? Shit was out of hand. I had to tell her what was going on and I had to be real with her. She would either help me or hurt me. Either way, I would learn if she was really on my side—if not, I could get her out of my life before it was too late; if so, then I had somebody I could depend on. The bottom line was that I had nothing to lose and everything to gain by telling Si-Si the truth.

"Si-Si, you want the real deal?" I said.

"I want the real deal."

"All right," I huffed. "The rumors about me being a transsexual are true and that's why I didn't go to no lawyers. Apparently O told the press as revenge for me not wanting to get back with him."

"*What?!*" Si-Si shouted. "Wait a minute! Hold the fuck up! Celess, are you fuckin' serious? Oh my God!"

I didn't say anything. I waited for Si-Si to calm down. I gave her time to register what I had told her and get past the shock. Then I wanted to see what her response was going to be.

"I don't believe this shit," she said. "What the fuck are we going to do?"

It was then that I realized that my instincts were right about Si-Si. I knew when I first met her that she was a rider; how she was handling my confession, she sure was. I then decided to tell her the whole entire story from beginning to end, all the way back to when Tina had first introduced me to dressing up as a chick in high school. I left out no details, telling Si-Si about how Tina and me used to run game on niggas everywhere we went, how we fucked dudes with a lot of money, and how most of them thought we were really girls. I told her about O, how we met, and how it turned out that he was an undercover fag and an undercover cop. I told her about him being in a witness protection program. I even told her about Michael and how I had just hooked up with him after he caught me snorting blow in a stairwell. I told her the whole truth about everything.

"You know what, that was some fucked-up shit O did. You just gonna have to fight fire with fire," she said.

"What you mean?" I asked her.

"You said that nigga was an undercover, right? And he's in hiding now 'cause he got some major players indicted?"

"Yeah," I said, thinking I knew where Si-Si was going but not really sure she was that damn crazy.

"Well then, the only way you gonna get his ass back and get him off ya shit is by puttin' his ass on blast like he did you. You in Philly right now, right?"

"Yeah."

"Well take ya ass over to Delaware." She paused and asked, "Delaware is right over there near Philly, right?"

"Um-hum," I said.

"Yeah, well take a trip over there and get up with his old friends. I'm sure there's one that slipped through the cracks out that motherfucker. It always is. Find 'im and put a little birdie in his ear. And if he a real nigga, he'll do the rest."

I remained silent even though I knew Si-Si was waiting for my response.

"Well?" she asked. "You with it?"

"I don't know how that's gonna solve my dilemma, though."

"You know that once a new story hits the headlines the old stories get thrown out the window. Well, as long as O keep feeding the press quotes and shit, they're going to hound you to find out the truth. But if O gets shut the fuck down, then they will forget about you and move on to somebody else's eating disorder or sex scandal or some shit. That's just how it goes. You have to take out the trash in order for the can to stop stinking."

"I don't know, Si-Si," I said, still not with having O's life put in danger.

Si-Si beefed up. "Celess, what's not to know? The nigga told the world your biggest, most sacred secret. And not only that, he's harassing you about it. The next thing you know, the paparazzi's gonna dig deep enough and prove the rumors are true. Then ya career is really gonna be over."

I thought it over and realized Si-Si was right. O was making a mountain out of a molehill and all because I wasn't jumping to be with him. That was some sucker shit and I ain't never been one to allow no sucker shit. Plus, he had gone too far. He knew how important my secret was to me and he knew that having it revealed could hurt my career, let alone get me killed. I was heated all over again, riled up, ready to go to Nebraska and bust the nigga's ass myself.

"So what you gonna do?" Si-Si asked.

"I'ma go to Delaware tonight."

"You got a strap?"

"No!"

"That lady you stayin' with don't have one in her house?"

"Ms. Carol? I doubt it."

"Well, shit, I got one in my house. Ain't nothin' wrong with havin' a burner in ya crib. You never know when you might need that motherfucker."

"You right, but I doubt if Ms. Carol got one. Anyway, I'll be cool. Them niggas is cool."

"All right," Si-Si said. "Well, can you please call a bitch and keep me posted? Don't leave me hangin' like you did. That wasn't cool."

"I won't." I gave her my word.

"All right, girl. I'll hold it down for you out here for as long as I can, but as soon as you take care of shit up that way, get back out here so we can get back at this money."

"I feel you. I need to—bad."

"You and me both," Si-Si said, slight desperation in her tone.

I hung up with Si-Si feeling light, like I had dropped fifty pounds. I guessed it was from getting so much shit off my chest and coming clean to her about all my secrets. That shit was weighing heavy on me, pulling me under like quicksand.

That evening, right after the sun had gone down, I borrowed Ms. Carol's car and drove the half hour to Delaware. Everything looked so different. You could tell I had been away for a while. I rode around the block O used to have one of his houses on; just like I figured, everybody was out. Which was specifically why I chose to go at night. You couldn't count on catching a nigga outside during the day in the summertime but when night fell, everybody and their mom would be outside.

I circled the block twice before finally parking and beeping my horn to get the attention of one of O's young bulls. I couldn't remember his name to save my life, but I knew his face. He was the same dude who had told me O had gotten kidnapped, and though he had grown up a lot since then he was still a young bull in my eyes.

He slowly approached the car, inspecting it along the way.

"Yo, what's poppin'?" he asked in a surprised-to-see-you mixed with what-the-hell-you-doin'-out-here tone of voice.

"You was O's homey, right?" I asked, just to be sure my eyes weren't deceiving me.

"Yeah. Why you askin'?" he asked, looking around as if he was paranoid.

Sensing his discomfort, I cut to the chase. "I'm not a cop like he was."

"What you talkin' 'bout?" he asked, dumbfounded. "That nigga got killed."

"I heard. But you know everything you hear ain't true," I said, cleverly introducing the topic of O being alive and well.

"I don't know what you talkin' about, but you soundin' crazy," the guy said, stepping away from the car.

"He was an undercover," I revealed. "He got a lot of people indicted. They faked his death to protect him and now he's in hiding. I got some information on 'im if you want it."

The guy looked at me, frowning like he was calculating something in his head. He told me to hold up and went over to the crowd of other guys who were out there. They exchanged words and him and two other guys came back to my car.

"What you got on that pussy?" one of the guys asked me.

I wrote O's address on a piece of paper and handed it to him.

"What you want for this?" he asked.

"Just a number to reach one of y'all if I need to."

The guy rubbed his goatee and started spitting out digits.

I stored them in my phone. "What's your name?" I asked.

"Raw," he answered. "That's all you want?"

I nodded. "As far as I'm concerned I don't wanna see none of y'all again."

"Well, if you ain't settin' us up, you won't have to."

"In that case," I said, "it was nice meeting you."

The guy nodded. "Good lookin' on this. He took my whole family down."

I put my hands up as if to say do what you gotta do. Then I put the car in drive and took off, switching the radio back and forth between Power 99, 100.3, and 96.5 the whole ride home, trying to block from my head the shit I had just done.

August 2007

A lot went on once I got back to L.A. I hired a publicist to redeem my name and we held a press conference to deny and dispel the rumors that had been disseminated across the country. We had a doctor state that I was a diabetic and that I was giving myself insulin at the time the infamous photo was taken of me injecting myself. Yeah, he lied, but he got paid good money to do so and it wasn't like he was harming anyone. Also during the press conference we revealed that I would be checking into Passages Malibu rehabilitation center. The explanation was that I had been so depressed after the rumors surfaced that I had turned to drugs. By the end of the conference, the press empathized with me, and instead of them ridiculing me and hounding me for photos, they were apologetic. Wearing a white pantsuit and a pair of reading glasses, I played my part and the one word that came to mind as I walked off the stage was *suckers*.

I did the rehab thing for close to two weeks and then checked myself out. I figured I had what I needed to take control back over my life. I moved out of the condo Derrek had gotten me—well, actually, when I returned to it the locks were all changed so I was really forced out of it. I didn't flip my lid over it, though, because Derrek had every right to do what he did. I had no business bringing my habit to his home, especially not the way I did. Derrek had been nothing but nice to me. He of all people didn't deserve that. I simply stayed with Si-Si until I found a new place. I decided on a unit in the Biscuit Company Lofts on Industrial Street. They were new and priced reasonably for all the hype that surrounded them. Plus, they were cute with attractive amenities including a pool, security, a café, and beautiful views.

In addition to moving, I changed my cell number and got a different PO box. I wanted to cut all ties to the past and start fresh. I also started working again, booking small gigs at first, like commercials and print ads. I did some catalog modeling too and a few runway shows for charity events. I was slowly getting my name back out there in a positive light and Si-Si followed. She booked more gigs as well. We were both excited to book a gig to do a test shoot together for *Playboy*. We jumped at the opportunity, but before we were scheduled to do it, we went to the spa to make sure our bodies were at their best.

Si-Si and I were at L'Auberge Del Mar Resort and Spa in Del Mar, California, indulging in everything from the

Chardonnay vitalite vinotherapy body scrub, wrap, and massage to the vitamin C moisture drench facial. We had been in there going on the entire day getting pampered and talking. We had just finished laughing about how we were going to pose like Charlie's Angels for the shoot when out of nowhere I felt a sense of sadness sweep over me and a single tear rolled down my face.

"What's wrong with you?" Si-Si asked, puzzled.

I shook my head, not wanting to talk about what I was feeling bad about. "Nothing," I said, wiping away the tear.

"Then why are you crying?" she asked. "We were just laughing and joking."

"I know. It's cool. I just thought about something, that's all."

"What?" Si-Si persisted. "What did you think about?"

"Nothing. I'll tell you later," I said.

Si-Si gave me a look and then left it at that. We got our body waxes and our pedicures and manicures and were sent on our way. We left the spa right before it closed at seven, feeling completely rejuvenated. However, the issue that had made me tear up in the spa remained and so did Si-Si's questions, so as soon as we got in Si-Si's Range Rover Sport, I had no choice but to let it out.

"I don't think we should have done that to O," I said. "We could have gotten him back in other ways. It just don't sit right with me that he could be dead because of us."

"I knew that's what it was," Si-Si said. "And I feel bad some-times too when I think about it. But the fact of the matter is you have to put yourself first. Sometimes in life it's the things that are necessary that you wish you could avoid. I know I've come across times like that before. It isn't easy turning your back on people who you once loved. But it's what has to be done. And it doesn't get any simpler than that."

Neither Si-Si nor I said anything more. We just continued on home in silence, me leaning my head against the headrest and zoning out and her taking sips of the water she had gotten from the spa while keeping her eyes glued to the traffic.

It was a gorgeous Saturday evening and I was on my couch eating ice cream and cookies watching the red carpet count-down to the Teen Choice Awards. I was keeping my eyes peeled, trying not to even blink so that I wouldn't miss Si-Si and David. David had been nominated and took Si-Si as his date. It was her first awards show that she would actually be on the arm of somebody rather than strutting in with me. I'd helped her choose, from the rack of dresses that David's styl-ist provided, an electric blue Roberto Cavalli mini. It was hot shit and with a price tag of eight thousand dollars it damn well better have been.

I was kind of jealous that I wasn't on the carpet but was sit-ting at home watching like a spectator. But my few producer friends who were attending were taking their wives and children. It was cool, though, because I needed some time out of the spotlight, some time to see things from the outside looking in, you know, some time to reflect.

Everybody was being interviewed on the carpet, from T.I. to Jessica Biel. So far I didn't have any negative comments to make about anybody's wardrobe. A few commercial breaks and a dozen celebrity interviews and photo ops later, Si-Si and David were nowhere to be found. But I certainly hadn't been watching for nothing. Sean and an actress whose name was on the tip of my tongue were hand-in-hand on the carpet. I knew she played on one of the nominated TV series, though. They interviewed her and asked if she and Sean were a couple and the bitch not only said yes, but held up her hand to show off a diamond engagement ring. The two of them were smiling happily as they glided down the carpet, glowing like a god and a goddess.

I was torn. I mean, don't get me wrong, I could in no way be mad at Sean. But I had to call him and let him know how I was feeling about finding out he was engaged on TV. I mean, maybe I was trippin', but I thought I at least deserved to be told by him.

"Sean, it's me, Celess. I'm calling to tell you congratulations first of all. I'm watching the Teen Choice Awards and I saw you on the carpet with your new fiancée. I was so shocked to see that you were engaged since I didn't even know about it, but anyway, I'm happy for you," I said on Sean's voice mail.

Unexpectedly, I got a call right back from him, but instead of him thanking me for congratulating him he was asking me not to call him anymore.

Taken aback, I asked, "It's like that now?"

"Celess, it's been like that since your publicity stunt with Cliff. Then while you were away shooting the movie it was all this talk about you being a man. I came to the conclusion that while I liked you a lot, you came with too much drama for me. And I'm sure I'm not telling you anything you haven't heard before. I've moved on and I hope you have too. So, out of respect for my new life, I'd appreciate it if you lose my number."

Click.

I looked at my cell phone to see if Sean had really hung up on me. I thought I would be angry as hell, but I actually was more surprised than anything. Then again, I had to respect where he was coming from. I did insert a whole lot of drama in Sean's life. How could I not have expected it to end on a bitter note? I turned off the television, not caring about missing Si-Si and David. Hell, Si-Si probably Tivo'd it anyway.

I went into my bedroom, removed the fake orchids from the vase on my nightstand, and placed them on my bed. I dug in the vase, feeling around on the bottom, and retrieved a folded-up brown paper bag. I took it in the kitchen, making sure to close all my blinds, shades, and curtains first. Then I sat at my kitchen table and opened the bag, removing its contents one by one. Neatly folding the bag back and placing it to the side, I opened the baggie of cocaine and poured it out onto the mirror. I separated the tiny white crystals into four rows using a razor, put one end of my straw in the front of the first row and the other end in my nostril.

Sniiiif. Sniiiifff. Sniiiifff. I snorted each row until there was no more coke left. I put everything back in the brown bag, took it back in my room, and put it back in the vase. I wiped off my kitchen table. Then I washed my face. I threw on some better-looking clothes than the lounge-around shorts and shirt I had on and left my house to go to a bar. *As long as it's on my terms,* I told myself, walking through the parking garage to the graphite-on-cranberry BMW 3 series coupe I had bought myself well before Derrek had given me the Jag. I got in the car, turned the key in the ignition, and drove off.

I felt like a shooting star zipping through the vibrant and busy streets of L.A. My hair blowing in the wind, my energy level raging, and my body feeling free as a bird, I turned up the volume on the radio and rode, mumbling the words to "Party Like a Rock Star."

September 2007

I didn't know what it was about Hollywood that made people want to fuck everybody they worked with but that's exactly what happened with Si-Si and me after the *Playboy* shoot in Beverly Hills.

We were looking over some of the shots that we had taken, giving our critiques, and the photographer and his assistant were making comments about our bodies that weren't necessarily professional. They weren't bold at first. In fact, they held back some, testing our limits. But when Si-Si and I flirted back and made some lewd comments of our own, they loosened up. They started talking about how horny our shoot made them in comparison to the thousands of other naked women they'd taken photographs of. Of course Si-Si and I knew they were running game. I mean, *Playboy* had most of the country's baddest bitches grace its pages. Si-Si and I were definitely among them but to say that we were sexier than them was pushing it.

We didn't care, though. We had ulterior motives too. A sexual relationship with them would stir up a lot of controversy and press if we were ever desperate enough to need it, so while Si-Si took the photographer in a back room, I ended up fucking the assistant, which almost turned out to be a disaster. I wasn't wet and couldn't get wet so I initiated anal sex. And as I was guiding his dick into my asshole, he grabbed my waist and pushed me up off him.

"Why are you making me fuck you in the ass?" he asked. "You know that's a sign that you're a man. Are those rumors that were going around about you true or something?"

I was so embarrassed and ready to fuck somebody up, but I knew that becoming defensive would send the wrong message. So instead, I laughed like that nigga had told the funniest damn joke I had ever heard.

After a short while, he too broke out into laughter.

"What's so funny?" he asked, chuckling.

"The fact that you would think for one second that all this belongs to a man," I said, seductively rubbing my fingers up and down my clit.

We shared another laugh before he pulled me on top of him and agreed to give it to me the way I wanted it—in the ass. When it was all done, Si-Si and I gathered our belongings and headed for the door. The two lucky men made us promise that our encounters would never get out to their wives. Si-Si and I promised them. We were more than willing to keep the guys' secret as long as they played their parts by sending us each a check in the mail, inviting us to all the events, and, most important, pushing us hard to the higher-ups so that we could be made Playmates. The check that a Playmate received, especially if she was Playmate of the Year, was a nice sum and well worth posing nude and fucking a nigga or two, on the real. Plus, it would be a good addition to our résumés.

"So how do you think we did?" I asked Si-Si.

"I think we did good," she said. "We made 'em cum in like ten minutes." She laughed.

I chuckled and told her, "I wasn't talkin' about that!"

Si-Si took her eyes off the road for a second and glanced at me as if she was trying to figure out what I was talking about. Then she blurted, "Ohhh, you was talkin' about the pictures?"

"Um, yeah," I said as if I was talking to an airhead.

Si-Si became cocky and said, "Oh, we killed that shit."

"I hope we get chosen," I said.

"We will and if we don't we'll cause a whole lot of ruckus."

I huffed and said, "If we make the cover, we'll be back on the map. I mean we're doing all right now, but *Playboy* would get us our male fans back."

"I know, right. We do need that crowd again."

Just then Si-Si's cell phone rang. She picked it up and looked at the screen.

"It's my mom," she volunteered.

She answered her phone, smiling and excited, probably expecting to tell her mom how our shoot had gone, but before she could say anything past hello, her expression changed drastically and I knew something was wrong.

I waited anxiously for her to hang up with her mom so that I could find out what had happened.

"She's dead," she mumbled. "My grandmom just died."

I didn't know what to say besides that I was sorry. I offered to drive the rest of the way home, but Si-Si declined. She told me she would drop me off and then go to the hospital, but I told her not to worry about me and to go straight to the hospital.

We got to Huntington and rushed up to the ICU where Si-Si's grandmom had spent her days since her stroke in March six months ago. Si-Si's mom was in the room, bent over on the hospital bed hugging her mom and sobbing uncontrollably. She was asking God why he had to take her mom. She was an emotional mess. I had to turn away to keep myself from crying. And Si-Si broke down immediately upon seeing her mom in the condition she was in. It was a very sad situation because I knew how much Si-Si loved her grandmom and her mom. She always made comments about them two being all she had in the world. I shed a tear or two, but mostly stayed strong for the sake of Si-Si and her mom. I tried to console them, even though I knew that there wasn't much I could do to make them feel better about their loss. But for what it was worth, I gave them my all.

I helped Si-Si plan her grandmom's funeral service. It was held at a small church in Pasadena that Si-Si's grandmom used to attend and give tithes to every Sunday. Si-Si's mom didn't participate. She was having a rough time dealing with her mom's passing and seemed to be very depressed. She attended the funeral but refused to go to the burial. Si-Si tried to talk her into it, but she said she couldn't watch her mom go in the ground. So Si-Si left her mom home and asked David to stay there with her, which was a good thing because had David gone the paparazzi would have followed him and they would have had a field day with what ended up happening at the burial.

Si-Si and I were standing in the front, closest to the casket. The other people there, including a few from Si-Si's apartment complex and the church, were standing behind us in a semicircle. The pastor was across from us on the other side of the casket, giving his final prayer.

There was a light breeze. It was cloudy out, but not dark. I was looking around the cemetery and noticed a black car driving up the hill, coming in our direction. We were the only people out there burying someone at that time so I figured the car had to contain others coming to pay their respects to Si-Si's grandmom. As the car got closer, it slowed down. An eerie feeling crept over me and my instincts told me that something wasn't right.

Before I could react, a barrage of bullets rang out from the car. Everybody at the burial started screaming and ducking, scattering in various directions. Si-Si and I both covered our heads with our hands, trying to run for cover. It was so much confusion and noise but through it all, just as the car screeched away, I heard a man's voice shout, "Payback's a bitch!" I glanced up at the car as it sped off and wondered who the hell could have been trying to kill somebody at a fuckin' burial.

When the car disappeared and we felt safe to get up, we all rushed to our cars to flee the scene. I called the police and told them what had happened and they said they would send a car out. Scared to remain there waiting for the cops to show up, I gave them my address and asked if they could meet me there. No one was hurt physically. But emotionally, Si-Si was crushed. Seeing bullet holes in her grandmom's casket as we peeled away in terror was enough to make her kill somebody, I could imagine. She couldn't understand why someone would shoot up her grandmom's burial in the first place. It was a mess.

The police met Si-Si and me at my building moments after we had gotten there. After hearing the story, the police officer asked if we knew of anybody who would want to do something like that and we said no. I didn't mention the shooters yelling, "Payback's a bitch." As far as I was concerned, that would have insinuated that we had done something to them first, and I wasn't about to incriminate us in any way. However, I did give the police a detailed description of the car including the fact that it had a Florida tag. They took a report and then said they would go to the burial site to initiate an investigation.

Once the police left and Si-Si's phone stopped ringing with people asking her if she was okay and what the hell happened, we tried to figure out who would have pulled a crazy stunt like that at a got damn funeral. We didn't tell her mom or David. For all they knew we were still at the grave.

"Who the hell would want payback on anybody at my grandmom's funeral? I can't see any of them doing shit to nobody!" Si-Si shouted after I told her what the shooter said.

She was sitting on my couch, her head laid back against the top. She had her hand over her face, continuously wiping the tears that formed in her eyes before they could fall.

"And you said they had a Florida tag on their car?"

"Yeah."

"You sure it was a Florida tag?" she repeated, a look of concern suddenly on her face.

"I clearly remember those oranges on the tag," I said. "Why?"

Si-Si paused and shook her head. "No reason. I was just trying to figure out who would drive from Florida to do some shit like that. But it could've been a rental car. You know rentals have all sorts of tags."

"Well, whatever the case, it wasn't payback on those people at your grandmom's funeral, that's for sure," I said calmly.

Si-Si's eyes widened and she gave me a look as if to say *I didn't do anything*. "Then who was it payback on?"

"It was payback on us. Si-Si, what if O's not dead? What if it was him who shot up the burial?" I guessed.

Si-Si jumped up off the couch and said, "It was O! Shit! You right! That's the only person it could be. So that would mean that the guy who you sent to get at O never made it, huh?"

I shook my head.

"You need to call that nigga and find out what happened. Shit, he could be settin' you up."

Taking Si-Si's advice, I dug through my pocketbook and pulled out my cell phone. I searched through my contacts and came across the guy's name.

"Hello, can I speak to Raw?" I asked, feeling funny asking the older-sounding woman who answered for a name like Raw.

The lady huffed and with a ghetto attitude said, "Raw ain't here. He done got locked up out Nebraska some damn where. I don't even know what the hell he was doing out there. But if you wanna leave ya name and number I'll tell him you called whenever he get around to calling me again."

"No, that's okay," I said, hanging up.

I looked at Si-Si and she looked at me. "It *was* O," I concluded. "That nigga who was supposed to do the deed got locked up—in Nebraska."

Si-Si rolled her eyes and said, "So the cops must be still watching his motherfuckin' back then?"

I nodded in agreement. "They probably intervened the minute Raw came through."

"This shit is crazy," Si-Si said, an expression of concern returning to her face. "We need to get out of town for a little while. There's no telling who these niggas are O got on our asses, how much they know about where we stay or nothing. We fuck around and we'll end up dead if we stay around this motherfucker."

"Where you think we should go?" I asked, still surprisingly calm.

Si-Si paced the floor. "What about that lady in Philly?"

I dialed Ms. Carol.

Ring! Ring!

"Hello," Ms. Carol answered.

"Hi, Ms. Carol," I greeted her, trying to sound as normal as possible.

"Celess, hey," she said. "I was just getting ready to call you."

"Oh, for real? Why? What's goin' on?"

"Some guy came by looking for you a minute ago."

"What guy?" I asked, extremely curious and worried.

"He didn't leave his name. But he was tall and dark-skinned," Ms. Carol described. "I told him you were back in L.A. and he said he would contact you. I told him to give me his information so that I could tell you he stopped by but when I went to get something to write on he left. But he did leave a letter at the door for you. I can open it and read it to you if you want me to," Ms. Carol informed me.

Completely unaware of who could have been looking for me in such a suspicious manner, I grew paranoid. I didn't want Ms. Carol to open the letter for fear that she would read something that I didn't want her to know.

"Oh, um, that's okay, Ms. Carol, you don't have to do that. I was planning on taking a trip up there soon anyway. I can read it when I get there," I said.

"Well, maybe I can just drop it in the mail to you," Ms. Carol suggested.

"Oh yeah, could you do that?" I figured that would be best. Now it seemed as if O had beat me to the punch and would possibly be there waiting for me when I arrived.

"Okay. So what's up? How's everything out there?"

"All right," I said. "Well, actually not quite. Si-Si's grand-mom passed. Her funeral was today."

"I'm sorry to hear that," Ms. Carol said. "Make sure you send my condolences."

"Matter fact, this is Si-Si on my other line," I lied. "Ms. Carol, I'm gonna have to call you back."

"Okay, honey."

"Bye-bye."

"What was that about?" Si-Si asked as soon as I took my ear away from the phone.

"Ms. Carol said that some guy came to her house looking for me—and the way she described him, it sounded like O."

Si-Si frowned. "This shit is gettin' a little bit too deep," she said.

"He must have sent somebody out here," I guessed.

"Does he have that kind of clout?" Si-Si asked.

"He did back when I messed with him. Who knows what he's working with now? And if the shit went down the way we think it did and the cops caught Raw in the act of trying to murder O, there's no telling what O is thinking. I mean I was the only person who knew his whereabouts other than his family and I was the only person who knew the niggas he used to deal with in Delaware. So all he had to do was put two and two together and figure it out that I had set him up. Either way, we're in trouble," I concluded.

"You think they know we're here?"

"I wouldn't doubt it. Shit, they knew where the burial was."

"We need to get out of town then, huh?"

"Definitely."

"You think we should go to Philly for a while until shit die down?" Si-Si asked, immediately going into plan mode.

I shook my head. "Not no more. He was in Philly looking for my ass. We can't go there," I reminded her. "What about ya hometown? You're not from here, right?"

"I did some dirt my damn self. It wouldn't be a smart move," Si-Si said quickly, sweeping that idea under the rug.

"Then what the fuck we gonna do, go somewhere we don't know shit about?" I asked, panic coming over me.

"I do have one place we might be able to lay low at," Si-Si said. "Do you have international calls on your phone?" she asked.

"No."

"We need to go get a calling card then," Si-Si said.

We carefully left my building and drove to a mini-mart close by. We bought a calling card and as soon as we got back in the car, Si-Si dialed a number from her phone.

Meanwhile, I was driving wondering about the extent of danger I was in and listening in on Si-Si's conversation to see how I might be able to get out of it. That's when I realized the bitch wasn't even speaking English. I swear, Si-Si is a damn chameleon. When she's talking to me she's ghetto fabulous like a motherfucka but let her be around some ritzy white folks or some damn Italians, you would think she graduated magna cum laude from a charm school. Bitch'll get to speaking different languages on ya ass and everything.

I couldn't understand a word she was saying, but she seemed overly happy so I guessed she had found us somewhere to go. I just had no idea how far.

"We can go to Rome," Si-Si said immediately after ending her international call.

"Rome?!" I asked, not sure if I was down to go that far.

"Yeah," she said. "Shit, we have to go somewhere. And it'll only be for a little while until O backs down."

"Well, what's a little while, 'cause I have bills to pay and stuff and I don't know about no Rome. I mean damn, Si-Si, you don't have family in the damn U.S.?"

"First of all you actin' like a mothafucka didn't just try to blow our brains out a minute ago! We really don't have a choice. Plus, the money we make over here is pennies compared to what we could make over there. This Hollywood shit ain't all it's cracked up to be . . ."

"You ain't never lied," I cut her off to cosign. "It's like a roller coaster; it takes you to the top slow as hell and drops you to the ground fast as fuck."

"It's for the birds, for real," Si-Si agreed. Then she went back to making her initial point. "The bottom line: what other choice do we have?"

She was right. We didn't have much of a choice. It was either go to Rome with Si-Si or stay in L.A., in the spotlight, and wait for O to catch up with me. And I loved my life too much to choose the latter. I mean I had been through too much and had come too far to have everything taken away from me over some nut-ass nigga who I *used* to deal with. I decided I would take my chances and go to Rome. It couldn't hurt. We booked three one-way tickets for the following week and hardly slept one night from then on.

October 2007

Si-Si and I had been paranoid since a week earlier when her grandmom's burial site was shot up. To avoid being injured or killed we stayed in public places where cameras and/or cops were in close proximity. Then the day arrived for Si-Si, me, and her mom to get on a plane out of the country. We had some things to do before we left for the airport at one-thirty that afternoon: I had to get the rest of my money out of the bank and Si-Si had agreed to get my mail for me, plus she still had to finish packing for her mom who hadn't done anything but eat and sleep since her mother's death. I felt sorry for Si-Si because she was burdened by it all, having to be the provider and the comforter without having anyone she could lean on for her own comfort. I tried to be that someone but she always fronted like she was fine.

I was on my way home from the bank when Si-Si called

my cell. She told me that she was outside my house waiting for me to get there so she could give me my mail. I asked why she didn't just keep it with her and give it to me at the airport. She added that she needed to borrow some of my luggage to put her mom's stuff in. I told her I would be at my building in five minutes. I got to my building and Si-Si and I went up to my loft. Once I reached my door, I noticed it was ajar. I pushed it open some more just enough to see that my house had been ransacked. Si-Si and I were scared to death. We didn't go inside, scared that whoever had done it was still inside waiting for me. We quickly ran back down to the parking garage and jumped in Si-Si's car, leaving mine behind. Neither of us knew what to do because we had to be at the airport no later than three to be able to check our bags and it was one-ten and I wasn't able to go home and get my stuff or the luggage for Si-Si's mom. We figured we would go to Si-Si's and at least get her stuff, grab her mom, and head to the airport. With so much security, at least we knew we would be safe there.

"Why is he doin' this?!" I shouted, unable to control my temper.

"We tried to have 'im killed. It makes sense that he would do this. I know I would," Si-Si said, as if it wasn't her outrageous plan to set O up in the first place. "You can't threaten someone's life and expect for them to just lie down and shut up about it."

"No shit, Si-Si. That's why I didn't wanna do that shit from jump!"

Meanwhile, Si-Si was driving through L.A.'s heavy traffic like a bat out of hell, cutting corners at like sixty miles per hour, causing everything that wasn't nailed down to shift or fall to the floor, including my pile of mail. I reached down to pick it up and Si-Si told me to leave it there. She said we didn't have time to be checking mail. She was right. Besides, I would have plenty of time to go through it on the plane.

We pulled up to Si-Si's apartment complex. Instead of parking in a parking spot, she parked alongside the curb close to the stairs that led to her apartment. We climbed out of the car and ran up the steps, watching over our shoulders. We arrived at Si-Si's door and it was closed and locked, so we didn't believe that we had anything to worry about. Si-Si opened the door with her key and walked inside. The house was spotless, everything was in its place, nothing seemed strange. Si-Si went straight to her mother's bedroom to get her out of the bed. Meanwhile, I stayed in the living room, peeping out of the window at Si-Si's car every now and again.

"AAAARRRRRHHHHH! AAAAARRRRHHHHH!" Si-Si's loud, piercing screams frightened me to the point that I was ready to jump out of the window.

I ran to the bedroom. Si-Si's mother was lying on the bed

in a pool of blood. She had been shot in the neck; there was a hole below her earlobe. Si-Si went berserk. She grabbed her mom, lifting her limp head off the pillow, trying to wake her. She was screaming, begging her to wake up. I was frozen stiff at the doorway watching it all. Si-Si cried until no end, finally releasing the tears that I knew had been bottled up inside her.

After a brief moment of being paralyzed with fear, my survival instincts kicked into gear.

"Si-Si, we gotta get outta here," I said, picking up Si-Si's luggage that was gathered at the doorway. "We have to go now!"

Si-Si didn't respond to me. She didn't even look up at me. She was still sobbing over her mom's dead body. I decided that I would leave her there for a minute while I took her bags down to the car. I figured I would do all the work and give her time to grieve and then once the car was packed up, I would drag her out of the apartment.

I power walked out of Si-Si's apartment and down the flight of stairs out to the car, carrying two duffel bags and a rolling suitcase, almost tripping down the steps on several occasions.

I went to open the trunk and realized that I didn't have the keys. I left the luggage on the sidewalk near the car and ran back up the steps, taking two at a time. I was almost at the top when I was stopped by a guy holding a gun to my face.

I flashed back to the last time I was staring down the barrel of a gun and I screamed for dear life. I just knew my time had come when I heard two deafening *pops*. My heart was beating at an abnormally rapid speed.

I opened my eyes slowly, afraid of what I might see, and there was a broken-down Si-Si lifting me up off the step. She was shaking uncontrollably as she tried to help me on my feet. It took me a while to grasp the fact that I hadn't been the one shot, but when I did, I praised God.

I looked past Si-Si, who was now in front of me, and saw the guy who just had a gun to my face lying facedown on the stairs right behind her. Blood poured from his back. He was still brandishing the gun he had planned to shoot me with.

Si-Si was crying and shaking, even more devastated than she was previously. I realized that I would be the one who had to take control of the situation.

"Si-Si, give me the gun," I told her, trying to be as calm as possible.

Si-Si handed me a small chrome-and-black gun that still had smoke coming out of the barrel. I ran it around to the Dumpster that was in the parking lot of the complex, wiping her prints off first before I threw it in.

"Where are your car keys?" I asked Si-Si as I ran back toward her.

Si-Si dug in the pocket of her cropped jacket and pulled

out her keys. I took them from her hand and unlocked the car doors. I helped her into the passenger seat and then dumped her suitcases in the trunk, opening one frantically and pulling out whichever items of clothing were on the top. I jumped in the driver's seat and threw Si-Si a shirt and pants. I ordered her to take off her clothes and put on the ones I had given her. I opened the bottle of water that was in the cup holder and poured some out on my hands and some on her hands.

"Try to get as much of that blood off you as possible," I told her, starting the car up and putting it in drive.

I stepped on the gas so hard, the car jerked and screeched. I sped away from the curb and headed toward LAX. A lot was going through my mind: had I done the right thing with the gun, and did I leave anything behind that might link Si-Si and me to the dead guy? I was worried to death thinking about it all, wondering if I could have done a better job cleaning up the evidence. But I knew that I couldn't have done anything more, especially since we had to get out of there as fast as possible. There was no telling if another gunman was on his way or even the police. And I had no intentions on Si-Si and me waiting around to find out.

By the time we got to the airport, Si-Si and I were both changed. Our clothes didn't match, but they weren't bloodstained. We put the car in long-term parking, checked Si-

Si's bags, and headed toward our gate. We had just a couple minutes before our flight was to board, but I had some burning questions and concerns, so I hustled Si-Si into the ladies' room before we got on the plane.

"Are you all right?" I asked her in a low voice.

Si-Si nodded. She went to the sink and threw water on her face, squeezing her eyes shut with each splash.

"I don't believe I just did that," she finally said, breaking her silence.

"You saved my life," I told her, trying to make her feel better. "You did what you had to do. That nigga was going to kill me."

"I know," she said. "But that wasn't O, was it?" Si-Si started pacing, squeezing her eyes shut as if she was thinking of a plan.

I shook my head and revealed, "No. O is dark-skinned with curly hair. That guy was light and bald-headed. I don't know who the fuck that was." I paused, and then it dawned on me that Si-Si never saw O so how did she know that wasn't him? "How did you figure that?" I asked her, needing to get to the bottom of the mystery.

Si-Si stopped pacing and started rubbing her hands through her hair. She leaned over, placing her palms on the bathroom sink. Looking down, she said, "It wasn't O who visited Ms. Carol's house looking for you."

"What do you mean? How do you know?"

"Because," she began, "and don't get mad at me when I tell you this, but when you sent me to get ya mail I read the letter that Ms. Carol sent you. It wasn't from O. It was from that guy Michael you told me about saying that he been trying to get in touch with you but your cell number was changed. He said he missed you and wanted to see you. And then I opened another letter that actually was from O; it was dated after the shooting saying how sorry he was for what he done, that he just felt slighted, like you were purposely pushing him off, but he figured you were probably really busy. It said that he was being relocated because somebody had tried to kill him and that as soon as he got settled he wanted you to visit him so he could make it up to you," Si-Si briefed me.

"Si-Si, what the hell? Why would you open my mail and keep something like that from me? And who the fuck was that tryna shoot me?"

She motioned for me to keep my voice down. "Honestly, Celess, I was scared and I didn't want you to leave my side if you found out that it was me them niggas was after rather than you."

As much as I wanted to stay in that bathroom and get the whole truth, our plane was about to board and so Si-Si and I had to rush to our gate. We sat in our first-class seats and didn't say anything about what had happened, fearful that someone would overhear and rat us out. We both remained tight-lipped as we closely watched everybody who boarded the plane. And believe me, it was hard as hell for me to keep my mouth closed. I had a thousand and one questions for Si-Si. I knew that girl had some secrets and there was no way I was continuing on with her unless they were revealed that day.

The Aftermath

I was looking out of the small plane window, staring at the beautiful, fluffy-looking clouds. I had drunk the last of my cranberry and vodka and watched Si-Si order her third when I decided to get to the bottom of our dilemma.

"Si-Si," I said.

She turned to look at me.

"What dirt did you do back in your hometown? Who are your enemies? I mean I'm gonna ride this thing out with you, because you my friend and you rode out my shit with me. But you have to be all the way real with me. I need to know what I'm up against," I said plainly, ready to hear all, hoping for the best but preparing myself for the worst.

At that moment, the stewardess handed Si-Si her drink. Si-Si thanked her and then gulped it down. She took a deep breath and said, "Well, I might as well start at the beginning."

I braced myself and prepared to listen intently. I hung

onto her every word, too, not wanting to miss a beat. Like I told her, I didn't have any ideas on abandoning her and leaving her to fight her battle on her own because that wasn't the case. I just had to know what problems we had and with whom before we landed and I stepped off the plane with Si-Si all the way on the other side of the globe.

"My real name is Sienna," she began. "I grew up in Miami, raised by a guy named Chatman who made millions in the sex trade. The guy we're going to see, Andrew, was one of my clients when I was a worker. He lives in Italy and he's the one who helped me . . ."

By the time Si-Si had finished telling her story she was in tears apologizing to me for getting me in the middle of her bullshit. I just reached down and placed my hand over hers, squeezing it firmly but gently.

"It's all right," I told her. "We gonna be cool. Us two together out in Europe? There ain't gonna be shit them niggas can do to us out there. I'm ridin', you hear me?" I tried to comfort her. It was the least I could do. That girl had been through some shit. And if she was right about who might be after us, then I was just thankful that we were still alive. I leaned my seat back and rested my head on the small complimentary pillow, closed my eyes, and counted my blessings. *Six more lives left*, I thought as I tried to force myself to sleep. *Let's hope I use them wisely*.

Acknowledgments

All praises be to Allah, first and foremost. You brought me far fast and I'm surely following your lead.

Thank you to Rich and Amir for holding me down always! I love y'all beyond words!

Thanks to my family and friends once again for everything! Y'all truly play y'all's parts each and every time!

Thanks, Liza and Sulay, for your never-ending belief in me and to my Liza Dawson Associates and Simon & Schuster families for guiding my career.

Thanks, Karen Quinones Miller, for your ongoing advice and mentorship.

Thanks, Marisol Thompson, for your assistance on this one.

Thanks to Dawn Michelle of Dream Relations, and to the newest edition Makeda Smith.

Thanks to people like Carol Mackey of Black Expressions, Heather of Disilgold, Heather and Alim of *Infinite* magazine,

Charles Gregory of 3 Guys Don't Lie, and the list goes on and on. Your support doesn't go unnoticed! I appreciate you!

To all the supporters, retailers, distributors, and readers, thank you for keeping me in the running.

And to my fans—thank you for bringing me this far! I'm five books in now! There's no way I could have done this without you!

If I've missed anyone, I sincerely apologize. I'll make up for it—I promise!

Ya girl,

Miosh

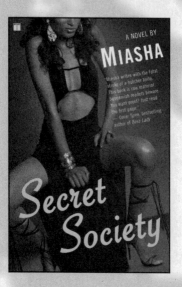